TWISTED JUSTICE

Jeffrey Ashford

Chivers Press   •   G. K. Hall & Co.
Bath, Avon, England   Thorndike, Maine USA

This Large Print edition is published by Chivers Press, England, and by G. K. Hall & Co., USA.

Published in 1994 in the U.K. by arrangement with HarperCollins Publishers Ltd.

Published in 1994 in the U.S. by arrangement with St. Martin's Press, Inc.

U.K. Hardcover ISBN 0–7451–2370–8 (Chivers Large Print)
U.K. Softcover ISBN 0–7451–2386–4 (Camden Large Print)
U.S. Softcover ISBN 0–8161–7409–1 (Nightingale Series Edition)

The text of this Large Print edition is unabridged.
Other aspects of the book may vary from the original edition.

Set in 16pt. New Times Roman.

Printed in the U.K. on acid-free paper.

British Library Cataloguing in Publication Data available

Library of Congress Cataloging-in-Publication Data

Ashford, Jeffrey, 1926–
    Twisted justice / Jeffrey Ashford.
        p.   cm.
    ISBN 0–8161–7409–1 (alk. paper : lg. print)
    1. Large type books.   I. Title.
[PR6060.E43T89   1994]   94–18221
823′.914—dc20

TWISTED JUSTICE

CHAPTER ONE

It was designated semi-desert mesquite savanna; a countryside so featureless that, unless one knew the Tumbleweed Proving Grounds lay ahead, it was difficult to understand why anyone had thought it worth his while to post the notice prohibiting access to the public beyond that point.

Leaving a trail of dust, the state patrol car drove along the graded dirt road that cut a Euclidean straight line through the undulating, parched, tired land, towards the glow on the horizon. Inside it, the four state deputies in their neat brown uniforms sweated even though the air-conditioning was holding the temperature to a pleasant level. It was by far the biggest and most dangerous job any of them had been on.

The car breasted a rise and the source of the glow became apparent—the compound on the eastern end of the proving grounds. One of the men made a sound like a hiccup, but it was not repeated. The road fell away and the compound was lost to sight.

They continued at a steady fifty, under the command of cruise control, despite the fact that the instinct of each of them was to drive as fast as possible in order to cut the waiting time. The success of their plan initially depended on their doing nothing to draw attention to themselves.

The land levelled out and the illuminated compound once again became visible, now in sufficient detail for them to make out the electrified perimeter fence, the administrative buildings, and the half-sunken bunkers. They visualized the defences—heat and movement detectors, guards on duty with loaded M2 carbines, relief guards, video cameras, satellite communication with the nearby helicopter base...

Standing orders laid it down that at all times one guard was on duty at the gates and the remaining three were in the guard-room, keeping a check on the monitor screens; at the first sign of trouble, relief guards were to be alerted and a call made to the nearby army base. Helicopters, loaded with troops, would be scrambled ... Rules were made to be ignored, especially when there had never been an incident and was never likely to be one. So after midnight on three nights a week, when pornographic films were broadcast by the local TV station, far more attention was given to the portable TV set (there contrary to standing orders) than to the monitor screens...

The driver, who wore sergeant's stripes, disengaged ride control and let the car slow down on the overrun. It came within the direct beam of the arc lamps which flanked the gates and each man felt as exposed as when he had

2

last stood against a wall, a plastic number board in his hand, and his photograph had been taken, full face and in profile. No guard was visible. The driver braked to a stop and, obeying the lower notice on the gate, turned off the engine.

The guard-post, which lay twenty feet back, was brick built; what was not immediately obvious was that the side facing the gates was lined with steel, as was the single door on the south side.

A guard, carbine slung over his right shoulder, small control unit in his left hand, came out of the hut and walked half way towards the gates. 'Yeah?' His expression reflected his annoyance at having his film-watching interrupted.

The driver lowered his window. 'It's about the crate.'

'What crate?'

'In the trunk. We want to know what's in it.'

'Then why not open the goddamn thing and find out?'

'Because we found it in a house we raided earlier on and it's marked Tumbleweed Proving Grounds. That makes the captain so shit-scared that he won't touch it until he's cleared to do so.'

'I ain't heard nothing's gone missing. They'd have surely been screaming loud enough for the dead to hear if there was.'

'All I know is that we've got this crate and

need to be certain what it contains.'

'Rubbish, most like.'

'Come on, man, find someone who'll give us the details and then we can go back and make everyone happy.'

'There's no one here but us guards and won't be until the morning. Return then.'

'The captain's not going to take that—even looking at it makes him shiver because this place is so goddamn secret it doesn't exist. What say we make it easy for everyone and leave the crate and you get someone to look at it in the morning?'

The guard, being of an ornery nature, would have argued had this not meant more time spent away from the television. 'All right, carry it in and dump it.'

'Are you kidding? It weighs a ton. Open up the gates and let us drive it up to where you want it.'

The guard pressed one of the buttons on his control unit and the gates opened, sounding a buzzer in the post that was just audible to those outside. The car drove through and parked where the guard indicated. The driver opened his door and climbed out. 'It's in the trunk.'

'So?'

The driver went round to the trunk and lifted the lid, effectively screening the rear of the car from the video camera by the gates. The guard moved until he could look at the oblong wooden crate. 'I don't see nothing to say it's

4

from here.'

'The marks are on the other side. Turn it over and you'll see 'em.'

'Don't the other three of you move?'

The driver smiled. 'They're on strike because they're not being paid overtime.'

The guard swore, tried to turn the crate and swore again when he found it too heavy to move with one hand. He put the control unit down on the roof of the car, unslung the carbine and did the same with that and then, leaning forward, took both hands to the crate. 'Come on, I ain't aiming to rupture myself.'

The driver moved, but instead of standing alongside the guard to help, he came up behind him and pinned his body against the lip of the trunk.

'Jesus! you're guillotining my belly...'

The driver, who'd brought a small can from his pocket, pressed the button to release a sickly smelling spray. The guard could make only a brief struggle before he collapsed into unconsciousness, his head striking the crate.

'Move.'

The other three scrambled out of the car, carrying paratroop Kalashnikovs with folding stocks; one was handed to the driver. They crossed to the guard-post, flung open the doors, raced inside, guns levelled. The twelve monitor screens were unwatched and the guards were grouped around the portable TV set, the alarm buttons and radio transmitter

5

well beyond their reach.

'Up against the wall.'

They did not obey immediately, trying, despite the sense of shock, to find a way of sounding the alarm. The muzzle of a Kalashnikov was pressed against the neck of the nearest guard. He stood and this decided the other two that any resistance was futile. The three of them crossed to the far wall. They were expertly tied up so that any attempt to struggle would tighten a loop around the neck, threatening to throttle the struggler.

One of the raiders remained in the guard-room, the other three left through the second doorway and went down the passage, past the wash-room, to the bunk-room. The overhead light was switched on and the sleeping men roughly awakened. Any resistance was so obviously ridiculous they quietly obeyed the order to file into the guard-room where they were tied up.

Three raiders left the hut and walked down the metalled road to the four rows of concrete bunkers, half sunk in the ground, separated from each other by protective walls. They stopped by No. 6. Steps led down to a heavy metal door, secured by a massive padlock. One of them used a set of skeleton keys with such skill that the padlock was forced within forty seconds. The door was made fast by cleats. When these were undone, it opened smoothly and easily, despite its considerable weight.

The driver switched on the overhead light. In the centre of the bunker was a stout wooden table and against the longer walls were shelves; the table had nothing on it and there were only three wooden boxes on the shelves. The boxes had rope handles, making it easy to lift them on to the table. Under the light, it was possible to read the marks on each and these included the word LAGSSAM.

The boxes were opened; each contained a shoulder-held, laser-guided, short-range surface to air missile launcher. In none of the boxes was a missile.

The driver swore. Intelligence had said that both launchers and missiles would be in the same bunker. Every extra minute they had to remain in the proving grounds raised the danger of being unable to make a clear getaway, yet a launcher without a rocket was virtually useless. He had learned over the years to curb his quick temper and to reason coolly under stress. There were thirty-six bunkers, in four rows; some might be almost as empty as this one; by the same token, some might be virtually full. If the rockets had been stored in a full bunker and the boxes containing them had not been marked sufficiently obviously for a civilian to recognize them immediately, it could take hours to identify them. They had one hour at the very most. So they couldn't make a complete search, only a partial one based on probabilities. What probabilities were there? That all who worked here would be no less energetic in doing as little as possible as their counterparts elsewhere. So if ordered to store launchers and rockets in separate bunkers, in the name of safety, they would choose ones as close together as possible ... 'Try five and seven first, then seventeen, eighteen, and nineteen.'

They carried the boxes out on to the road, entered bunker No. 5. This was almost full of equipment. Since most of the stencilled labelling was meaningless jargon to them, they had to smash open case after case to check on the contents. There were only twenty minutes left when they'd satisfied themselves that the rockets weren't in that bunker.

'No. 7.'

It was empty.

They crossed the road to the next line of bunkers, knowing that they could probably only try one more. The driver would never have admitted it, but he did believe in lucky numbers and on his eighteenth birthday he'd carried out his first successful heist. 'Eighteen.'

The other two didn't argue, but they were smelling failure and wanted to clear off and disappear before things started happening...

The shelves were half-full of boxes and crates, none of which carried the magic letters LAGSSAM. Where there was more than one box or crate of the same size and with the same identification, only the first had to be checked, yet even so, fifteen minutes had passed before they moved down to the second shelf. Then they found four rockets, in one of three similar boxes, seven inches long, four inches in diameter at the widest point, with noses painted red and six fins painted green. They would have recognized them from photographs, but this was unnecessary; each rocket had stencilled on it, just for'd of the fins, LAGSSAM.

They were contracted to provide six rockets; the extra six were an unexpected bonus.

*   *   *

They drove out through the open gateway and down the dead straight, undulating road, their headlights carving a path through the dark. When they were half way to the interstate highway, a message came through on the car's radio to ask if anyone in the past hour and a half had had contact with Three One. Their stolen patrol car was Three One.

They crested a shallow rise to come in sight of the highway, marked by moving lights; even at that hour of the morning there was considerable traffic. Half a mile short of the road, they turned off into the yard of a deserted house and parked alongside a three-year-old Chevrolet.

In the trunk of the Chevrolet were clothing, two cans of gas, and a small fire-bomb primed with a timer. They emptied the trunk, filled it with the launchers and rockets, changed into the civilian clothing, dropped the uniforms on to the seats of the patrol car, doused them with gas, set the bomb.

They drove off in the Chevrolet and once on the highway headed south.

*   *   *

There was a no-questions-asked motel just outside Aitchison, which lay four miles north of the border. They drove past the office, in which the clerk was slumped in a chair, snoring, and along to the two cabins previously booked. They parked the Chevrolet in the carport of the first. The driver took a 50-centavos coin and dropped it on to the carpet at the back, then scuffed it under the front seat with his shoe.

In the carport of the second cabin was a battered Ford on Mexican plates. Once the launchers and rockets had been transferred into the trunk of that, they drove off, heading west and running roughly parallel with the border. Ten miles on they reached the hills and in a convenient off-road clearing among the trees, they changed the Mexican plates for Arizona ones.

*   *   *

The fire was reported over an in-car telephone and a patrol car was ordered to investigate. The two-man crew found the missing Three One a flaming wreck, far too hot to be closely approached. As he stared at it, the driver wondered why someone should steal a patrol car, drive it there, and torch it, and came to one obvious answer.

Back behind the wheel of the patrol car, he radioed in and asked if there had been any alarm from the proving grounds. There hadn't. For many, that would have been good enough. But he had a dogged nature. 'We'll check out the grounds.'

'But you heard 'em say...'

He started the engine. Fifteen minutes later, when he made his report from within the grounds, all hell was let loose.

*   *   *

The Chevrolet was found in the motel carport and was driven to police HQ, there to be checked for prints and searched. The 50-centavos coin was found. That, together with the proximity of the border and the motel staff's evidence that two adjoining cabins had been booked by a man who drove a car with a Mexican number and who had spoken Spanish to his companion, convinced them that the raid had been organized from either South or Central America, with Bolivia being the most

11

obvious choice.

Forty-one hours after the raid, word came through from Tumbleweed Proving Grounds that a check showed three LAGSSAM launchers and twelve rockets had been stolen.

'What the hell's a LAGSSAM?' the sergeant asked over the phone.

'A short-range, laser-guided, surface to air missile. The laser sight has been under intense development.'

'So is it important?'

It was very, very important. Against helicopters, it was proving itself to be a deadly weapon.

The news was received with dismay by anti-drug enforcement agencies as well as the police. Helicopters were used in large numbers in Bolivia, Ecuador, Peru, and to a much lesser extent in west Brazil and Argentina, in an effort to eradicate the growing of the coca shrub and the manufacture of cocaine and if these could be easily shot down, the whole operation was in serious danger.

Anti-drug enforcement agencies throughout Central and South America were warned of the threat presented by the stolen LAGSSAMS.

CHAPTER TWO

The village of Carlington stretched across the top of a gentle hill; from some of the houses it was possible on a clear day to see the Channel. Torring Farm was to the south and below the hill. In the early 'fifties it had consisted of twenty-five acres of farm land, a one-acre coppice, a pond that was home to two kinds of newts, an Elizabethan farmhouse with peg-tile roof, and three tumbledown sheds. Then the owner had died and his only son, who had wisely forsaken farming for accountancy, had put the property up for sale. It had been bought in order to build an open prison on the site. The local opposition had been ferocious but, as always, the wishes of those most concerned were least consulted. However, as a sop to the opposition, the pledge had been given that no man found guilty of a crime of violence would ever be held there. The pledge was honoured for just over two years which, for authority, was a long time.

Either by chance or design, successive governors were of the liberal, progressive mould, viewing imprisonment a means of rehabilitation as much as punishment. When the number of visiting days were doubled, families were welcomed and toys were provided for children. Villagers renamed the

13

prison Torring Farm Rest Home.

There were two visiting rooms (as the large areas were called) and these were brightly decorated; on the walls of one, an Arcadian mural had been painted by a man who had murdered and dismembered two women. The furniture was arranged so that each family group could enjoy the illusion of some privacy. The warders wore civvies and were under orders to make themselves as inconspicuous as possible.

Illmore, his lean, sharply featured face with high cheekbones suggesting strength with little warmth, sat facing a blonde woman, younger than he, who attracted more than one admiring glance. With her was a young girl who wore a green party-style dress with many flounces. 'So how's Dave getting on?' he asked. His voice held an accent that was difficult to identify.

'Fine,' the woman answered.

'He's the gift of the gab, has Dave, which is what they like in the States. How long's he going to be staying there?'

'He's not saying yet.'

'Bit of trouble, is there?'

'Nothing like that. But he says he can't hurry back if he's to make things run smoothly.'

'That's fair enough. So what about Kate?'

'It's her party this evening.'

'Is that so? I wouldn't mind going to that! If I know Kate, it'll be going most of the night.'

'It's got to stop at one sharp on account of

the neighbours.'

'Since when's she bothered about them?' He laughed.

She spoke to her daughter who was playing with a doll, one of the toys provided by the prison. 'Cathy, come and sit on my lap.'

'Why?'

'So you can have a talk with Uncle Roger.'

'Who's him?'

'Don't be stupid.' She realized from Cathy's expression that she'd spoken far more sharply than she'd intended, looked quickly at the nearest warder and was relieved to note he was not watching them, reached out to Cathy and cuddled her before lifting her up on to her lap. 'Now tell Uncle Roger...'

'I want to play with Cindy.'

'Play with her while you tell Uncle Roger what you did yesterday.'

'I didn't do anything.'

'Of course you did. You went to the shops and bought him a present.'

'No, I didn't.'

'You really are being a muffin.' She opened her handbag and brought out a Mars Bar. 'You specially said you wanted to buy this to give to him, didn't you?'

'I want it.'

The nearest warder was watching them now. She smiled at him. 'My Cathy brought this for her uncle.' She held up the Mars Bar. 'Is she allowed to give it to him?'

Even in so liberally run an establishment, the rules laid down that no visitor was allowed to hand anything to a prisoner. But a Mars Bar? 'Why not?' said the warder, who had a daughter of about the same age.

'Give this to Uncle Roger,' she said, as she handed the bar to her daughter.

Cathy gripped it very tightly. 'I want it.'

'That's being very greedy.' She looked up and said to the warder: 'Don't you agree, Cathy's being very greedy?'

'I wouldn't say that, missus. Never have met a nipper who didn't look after herself first when it comes to sweets!' He smiled.

She said to her daughter, her tone firm, but not sharp: 'Show what a nice girl you really are and give it to your uncle.'

After a moment Cathy climbed down, crossed to where Illmore sat, looked hard and long at the Mars Bar in her right hand.

'That's a lovely present,' said Illmore.

'It's my favourite of all.'

'Then maybe you'd like some?'

'Yes. Lots.' She finally handed him the bar.

Illmore laughed. He unwrapped the bar, broke it into two unequal portions, dextrously wound the strands of toffee on to the larger piece, handed that back to her.

Through the PA system there came the chimes which marked the end of visiting hours. The warders sharpened their vigilance. This was the big danger point—under the cover of apparently overwhelming emotions, wives and girlfriends sometimes tried to pass things through forbidden embraces.

She reached out and drew Cathy, still facing Illmore, to herself. Her handbag was open on her lap and from it she brought out a small package that was wrapped in the same material as Cathy's dress; she dropped the packet into the 'pocket' which had been fashioned on the inside of one of the flounces. She gave her daughter a push. 'Say goodbye to Uncle Roger. Give him a kiss.'

Illmore gathered up Cathy and settled her on his lap. 'Now, do I get a really big kiss?'

The nearest warder watched approvingly, having far too much common sense to imagine that the rule against physical contact could be meant to apply to a young niece.

Cathy, after a slight hesitation, gave Illmore a chocolatey kiss on the cheek. He lifted her down, careful to make certain that she faced the nearest warder. 'She's as bright as a button,' he said.

'I can see that,' replied the warder.

'Say goodbye to Mr Fleming.'

'Who's Mr Fleming?' Cathy asked.

'I am,' said the warder. 'So do I get a kiss?'

'No.'

He laughed. 'Very wise of you.'

The warder's attention was on Cathy. Illmore lifted out the package from the 'pocket' in Cathy's dress. The woman stood, immediately drawing the warder's attention. Cathy crossed to her mother's side.

'It's been great seeing you,' Illmore said. 'Will you be here next Saturday?'

She nodded. Ironically, now that the transfer had been successfully made, she was far more scared than she had been before.

'You'll bring Cathy?'

'Yes.' Her voice had become croaky.

'You'd better start moving,' said the warder pleasantly.

Prisoners made their way to one end of the area, visitors to the other. As he waited by the doorway to pass through, Illmore felt the gun in his right-hand trouser pocket and knew fierce contempt for the sentimental warder.

*   *   *

The prisoners slept two to a room—the word 'cell' was not used—and this contained two beds, two chairs, a bookcase, a table, two cupboards, a handbasin, and a wall-mounted speaker with a control that gave a choice of radio programmes. There were no bars over the window and the door was unlocked, but between lights out and six-thirty in the morning a prisoner was only allowed to be outside his room if he needed help or to go to the lavatory.

Illmore looked at his watch, the hands of which were visible in the light which came through the uncurtained window from the inward pointing arc lamps along the perimeter fence. Twenty to one. Ten minutes before he moved. Timing was everything...

He slid carefully off the bed, yet even so the springs creaked. In the other bed, Branson stirred. Should he wake up, he'd have to be dealt with ... His breathing resumed its heavy evenness. Illmore checked the gun; compared to most, this snub-nosed .22 automatic was little more than a toy, but it was still a deadly toy.

He did not dress. To be seen clothed in the middle of the night must be to excite suspicion. He crossed to the door, opened it a couple of inches, and listened. The warders were meant to patrol the corridors throughout the night, but since each corridor was covered by a TV camera, those on duty spent most of their time in one or other of the control rooms.

He retied the cord of his pyjama trousers as tightly as possible to hold the gun at his waist, let his pyjama coat hang loose so that it concealed the butt. He stepped out into the corridor and walked with easy confidence— one could not judge whether a warder was watching a monitor screen...

In the square at the end of the corridor was a control room. It contained a bank of monitors, a table and chair, and a panic button, painted bright red. Atherton, one of the more pugnacious warders, was seated at the table on which were a box half-full of sandwiches, a Thermos flask, and a mug. Illmore was half way across the square when he turned. 'What's up with you?'

Illmore did not answer until he reached the open doorway. 'I've a bellyache, Mr Atherton.'

'Shouldn't eat so much caviar.'

The monitors showed all the corridors under surveillance to be empty. Illmore said in an ingratiating tone as he stepped inside: 'You wouldn't have some stomach tablets?'

'That's right, I wouldn't.'

'I really need something, Mr Atherton. It's hurting like someone had stuck in a shiv.' He took another two paces forward. Now, he was not very much further from Atherton than Atherton's right hand was from the button. 'It could be appendicitis. If it bursts...'

'You'll croak. Which'll save the taxpayers a fortune.'

'I must have something from the dispensary.' Another pace forward.

'Try a dose of arsenic.'

Atherton was becoming annoyed and annoyance could easily generate suspicion. Rather than try for another foot and a half, Illmore whipped out the automatic.

Atherton was no coward and he reached for the panic button.

'Press it and you're cold.'

He remained motionless, his right forefinger

just above the button. Then he slowly withdrew his hand. Heroes died young and their wives poor.

'Stand up.'

He stood.

'Turn round and start walking.'

They left the control room and went down the right-hand corridor to an outside door.

'Unlock it.'

'I haven't a key.'

'You've five seconds to find one before I stick the gun between your legs and turn you into a eunuch.'

He brought a bunch of keys out of his right-hand coat pocket and, with hands that were beginning to fumble, unlocked the door. A steel staircase led down to the ground. The muzzle of the gun dug into the back of his neck, telling him to start going down.

At the foot of the stairs there was a tarmac path which, bordered by flowerbeds on the far side, led round to the gates. They walked, brilliantly outlined by the arc lamps.

'They'll never open 'em for you,' said Atherton, as he neared the gates.

'They will if they know you're dead if they don't.'

The gates were remote controlled. Illmore stopped ten feet away, then addressed the camera which, atop of the right-hand gatepost, had been following them. 'Open up or I shoot, starting at the bastard's ankles and then moving up.'

The seconds ticked by. Then there was the low whirr of an electric motor and the right-hand gate began to open. As he forced Atherton to precede him, Illmore envisaged the control room at county police HQ. Already the call would have gone out to patrol cars to converge on the prison; if the police had access to a helicopter which could be used at night, that would soon be taking to the air...

The road—more lane than road—was bordered by a rough grass verge. He ordered Atherton to a stop on this.

'You'll not get any further.'

'For your sake, you'd better hope I do.' Illmore stared up the hill, willing the car to appear...

Headlamps cut the darkness, then bore down on them, partially blinding them. A black Jaguar came to a rocking halt. Illmore slammed the butt of the gun down on Atherton's head; Atherton buckled, but did not fall, yet was powerless to make any move.

Illmore scrambled into the back of the Jaguar and the driver accelerated away, holding the scrabbling tyres with constant work at the wheel. Fields and the occasional house flashed past them; at one point the winding lane rose sufficiently to offer a brief view out to the distant coast and the flashing white light of a lighthouse.

The driver braked hard, swung the wheel

over. They bounced their way along a rough dirt track that cut through a belt of trees to reach a clearing in which stood a grey 735 BMW. As they stopped, the front near-side door of the BMW opened and a woman climbed out. She switched on a torch to guide them across the uneven ground. 'Christ, you've been long enough!'

They were half a minute ahead of schedule. Nerves played havoc with time. In the back of the BMW were a dark suit, shirt, tie with regimental-style stripes, socks, and shoes. While Illmore changed out of his pyjamas, the driver put on a chauffeur's coat and peaked cap. If they were unlucky enough to be stopped, smart clothes, a loving woman, and a chauffeur, should paint a picture of innocence.

They drove back to the lane and continued south. After a while they began to relax. They were beyond the probable immediate search area. The driver switched on the radio and found some light music; the woman waited for Illmore to start pawing her, making up for the past months; Illmore watched the time, making certain they didn't relax to the extent that they failed to reach the waiting boat before it had to set sail.

The BMW rounded a corner, lurched and began to weave badly. The driver braked to a halt. 'It's a bloody puncture.'

Illmore knew a sudden rage. A carefully planned, expertly carried out escape, brought to a sudden halt because of something as minor as a puncture...

'Bring the torch over so as I can see what I'm doing,' said the driver.

He climbed out and stood by the offside wheel, holding the beam of the torch on it. The driver, cap and jacket off, jacked up the car, removed the punctured wheel, bolted on the spare, lowered the car. It was immediately apparent that the owner of the BMW, stolen the previous day, was not sharp on car maintenance—the spare was virtually flat. 'That's it, then,' said the driver and in his frustration he threw the jack at the hedge.

'Drive on with it as it is.'

'Are you a bleeding nutter? That tyre'll peel off as if it was a banana.'

'Find an all-night garage and pump it up.'

'Sure. There's one round every corner.'

'I said, drive.'

'And I said, not bleeding likely.'

Illmore jammed his hand into his coat pocket and gripped the gun. Then, accepting the futility of that, he swung round, crossed to the driving door, opened it, and sat behind the wheel. He started the engine and, ignoring the shouts of the other man, drove off.

'What are you doing?' the woman in the back demanded shrilly. 'You can't leave Bill back there.'

He ignored her. He had to reach the boat so that they could sail and be in international

24

waters before the authorities could react and block the coast. Until the puncture there'd been time in hand, now that credit was rapidly disappearing. He increased speed, despite the way the car began to lurch and snake. Petrol stations on the motorways were open twenty-four hours; he'd never had occasion to find out, but surely they had air lines? 'Where's the next motorway access?'

'For God's sake don't drive so fast...'

The tyre deflated and he failed to react quickly enough. The car swerved violently, slammed into the grass verge, and rolled with whiplash force. He'd not fixed the seat-belt and was thrown around like a feather in a storm. Half way through the second roll, his head smacked into something and he lost consciousness.

*   *   *

The world returned, retreated, returned, this time to stay. He wished to God it would retreat once more and leave him in the peace of nothingness. Consciousness meant pain; stabbing, searing pain...

His scrambled, aching thoughts slowly began to coalesce. He realized he dare not just lie there in a huddled heap, supinely waiting for help. He had to move and move fast ... Moving was agony, moving fast impossible...

He dragged himself to an upright position

and found he was out of the car, lying in a ditch. More time passed and then he was able to crawl over to the car which lay on its side, look into the back to see if the woman had fared better than he and was in a position to help him. He could make out nothing. The door had flown open as they rolled and had then been bent back so that now he could slowly ease himself up and over and with an even greater effort reach inside. His fingers met nothing but the car. She had not been as badly injured as he and had fled, leaving him to his own future...

He pressed the button on his wristwatch to illuminate the dial. The hands told him something he did not want to believe. There could be no escape for him tonight, even if he could pull himself together ... Then what? By now, someone in authority would have put two and two together and realized that his armed escape turned suspicions into fact. An all-out, priority search for him would be organized just as quickly as possible. So he dare not seek medical help or use any public place. Yet injured, bloody, dishevelled, he couldn't hope to escape notice, let alone remain at large to organize a second attempt to escape the country. But he had to, no matter what, because of what rested on his succeeding...

Very occasionally, he decided, a man could find himself in a position where he had to risk triggering one disaster because it was less potentially disastrous than another...

CHAPTER THREE

Andrew Stone half awoke to scratch his nose.
He realized the light was on and opened his
eyes to see that Joanna was holding a feather
an inch away from the tip of his nose. 'What
the hell?'

'Do you know that you sleep like a drunken
log?'

'Just an exhausted log.'

'No stamina, that's your trouble.' She
dropped the feather, leaned forward and rested
her breasts on his chest, kissed him with an
agile, exploring tongue.

He slid his hands down her back.

She freed her mouth. 'Cool it.'

'You did the warming up, not me.'

'Keep it on simmer for another time. Right
now, you've got to move.'

'Why?'

'Because Dad's so old-fashioned that he
objects to an unexpected breakfast guest.'

'Breakfast's still a long way away.' His
hands became busy again.

'Stop it, you bastard.'

'I have a full birth certificate to prove I was
lawfully conceived of parents who would never
have considered a romp on the hay before they

were married.'

'I'll bet they knew all about romps. You're going to stop and leave.'

'And forgo a trip to Arcady, Nirvana, and all stations to Shangri-La?'

She reached down to push his hands away, but did not exert very much force. 'Isn't Nirvana filled with houris?'

'I hope so.'

'Then you can leave that out of the itinerary.'

'Scared I'll be kidnapped?'

'You're so big-headed ... Stop it. That's not nice.'

'How would you know until you've tried it?'

*   *   *

Andrew left her bedroom and, shoes in one hand and small pencil torch in the other, crept down the corridor past her father's suite. He reached the door lined with green baize (the cordon sanitaire he called this, to Joanna's annoyance) and went through to the servants' quarters. He relaxed. The Portuguese couple, the only domestic help who now worked in the house, were away for a few days and it was impossible to imagine Joanna's father appearing in the area just before daybreak.

Downstairs, the very elaborate alarm system had been divided into units which could be individually isolated. This way, one could walk around in one part of the ground floor without trouble, while the slightest movement elsewhere would trigger the alarm. He switched off the unit which covered the butler's pantry, silver-room, housekeeper's room, and kitchen, then the one which covered the outside door by the game larder and the gates of the courtyard. In a few moments Joanna would come downstairs and reset them.

There was no moon, but the sky was clear and there was just sufficient visibility for him to be able to move without a torch. He crossed the courtyard to the gateway, very carefully opened one gate to slip through, then stepped sideways so that he could continue on grass and not the gravel drive—Joanna said her father had excellent hearing. He took two paces forward, stopped abruptly because he had the impression that there'd been movement to his right. He half turned, but because he was now facing the high brick wall, the darkness was too intense to make out anything. Then there were sounds, seemingly only inches away. Instinctively, he switched on the torch and in its small beam he caught a brief glimpse of a man whose face was dishevelled and bloody just before something smashed down on his head.

*　　*　　*

He registered consciousness to find his head

was filled with fire and it was some time before that subsided sufficiently for him to drag himself to his feet. The only reasonable explanation of events that occurred to his confused mind was that he'd run into a would-be burglar—would-be, since the dark, silent house surely meant there'd been no alarm? ... The back door. There had to be the possibility that the burglar had reached that before Joanna had gone downstairs to lock it and reset the alarms ... The back door proved to be locked. He remembered his father's telling him that ninety-nine burglars out of every hundred left a window or door open to provide a rapid means of emergency escape and he walked round the house. There was now just enough light for him to make out that every ground-floor window and door was shut. Satisfied that his assailant had been panicked by the meeting, he turned away and crossed the lawn, making for his motorbike which was hidden in a coppice a few hundred yards down the road.

CHAPTER FOUR

'My God, it's ten to eight!' June hurriedly sat upright in bed.

'Relax, love,' Stone said. 'It's Sunday, for once I've the whole day off, and if we want to stay in bed all morning, we can.'

'I'd forgotten.' She settled back.

'So I gathered when I found you fast asleep at seven despite the fact that you swear you always wake up at the crack of dawn.'

'I do. But for once I managed to get back to sleep, which is why I've overslept; or rather, I would have done if I could, but I couldn't as you don't have to go to work.'

'Female logic!' He chuckled.

'Sometimes you become insufferable!'

'A whole day off always goes to my head.'

There was a silence which she broke. 'Gerry, Andy didn't come home until just after five. That's far too late.'

'By whose standards? You've really got to start remembering that he is over eighteen and therefore in the eyes of the law a responsible adult.'

'I don't care about the law, he shouldn't be out so late.'

He wondered if she'd ever learn to control her protective instincts? Probably not since, when younger, she'd been so emotionally scarred. She wanted to clutch her family so tightly to herself that had they been unresisting, she would have been in danger of stifling them.

'What can he have been doing to come back so late?'

'Tom-catting, of course.'

'That'll only lead to trouble.'

'The dreaded pattering pubic parasites, pregnancy, and pox? . . . Andy knows the score, so he's got to be left to learn the hard way. No double meaning intended.'

'It's not a sniggering matter.'

'I'm not sniggering, merely trying to make you understand that when it comes to his sex life, our advice has become superfluous.'

She turned to lie on her back, stared up at the ceiling. 'It's her fault.'

'Who are you blaming?'

'Who d'you think? Joanna.'

'There is quite a dish!'

'How damned typical! Being male, all you can see is the image.'

'So what do you suggest lies beneath that?'

'She's been spoiled rotten and only considers herself and when she becomes bored with him, she'll throw him aside like a worn glove. From the beginning, it's been her leading him astray.'

'I rather think the idea of leading astray has gone by the board. These days, women are abreast of men all the way.'

'I suppose you keep making these smutty remarks because you think they're clever?'

'Once again, no double meaning intended.'

She was, he thought, making herself out to be a prude, yet she was very far from one. What she was really saying was that she was worried that in the weeks to come, Andy would be emotionally hurt. 'You know, I don't think things with him are as serious as you imagine.'

'Then you don't understand your son. And you certainly don't understand that she's leading him on because just for the moment she finds it amusing to go slumming.'

'That's ridiculous.'

'Have you been so completely taken in by the pretty face and curvy body?'

'Love, you're beginning to sound rather silly.'

He seldom criticized her and so his words jolted her. She said, in a small voice: 'Do you really think I am or are you just being argumentative?'

'She's from a rich background, sure, and probably hasn't ever before set foot in a semi-detached, but for my money that sort of thing doesn't mean much to her. She's too intelligent to be a snob. And in any case, these days the young aren't nearly so conscious of such things as we are or our parents were.'

'I wonder if you aren't kidding yourself? D'you imagine her father would welcome Andy as a son-in-law?'

'Don't you think he's good enough for her?'

'Or course I do.'

'Then why shouldn't Ogilvy think the same way?'

'Because he's her father, not Andy's. The rich are always scared that people are after their money and so they're afraid of the poor.'

'We're not poor, we're Mr and Mrs Average. And you're jumping fences before the race has started. Ten to one, marriage is the last thought to enter either of their minds.'

'More typical male reaction!'

* * *

All the semi-detached houses in Potters Road had been built in the late 'thirties by the same firm and to the same design, but various owners had made so many alterations and additions that now that fact was not immediately obvious.

Stone would never have described himself as an enthusiastic gardener, more someone who liked to see a garden looking neat and colourful; it was a difference which did not add up to much when it came to the work. He was in the small aluminium-framed greenhouse at the bottom of the garden, cursing the whitefly which seemed to thrive on insecticide, when Andrew came down the narrow gravel path to stand in the open doorway. 'You look like you had a really heavy night,' he observed.

Andrew made no reply.

'I take it someone is wielding a five-pound hammer in your head and someone else is stomping around in your stomach in hobnail boots?'

'I wasn't on the booze, Dad.'

Stone was glad of that. He'd all too often had to deal with the tragic consequences of drunken driving and could never quite escape the fear that one day Andrew would have that one beer too many and then drive ... 'So why the resemblance to a corpse?'

'Last night, something bloody odd happened. I was ... If I tell you something, will you keep it quiet from Mum?'

'I don't think I can agree to that without knowing what it is I'm to hide.'

'It's only because ... She'll get upset. She doesn't seem to like Joanna.'

'Accept the fact that she'll never approve of any girl you bring back to the house who isn't a paragon of all the virtues. And if ever you meet such a girl, my advice is to move on quickly before you're bored to death.' He had expected a quick smile, but Andrew's expression remained worried. 'What's the problem?'

'I ...' Andrew began to jingle some coins in the pocket of his jeans. 'I was with Joanna last night. I didn't leave her place until quite late.'

'Your mother says it was just after five when you got back.'

'Yes, well ... We kind of lost track of the time, so when I left I had to go out through one of the back doors...'

Stone was amused by Andrew's embarrassment. Perhaps the modern generation were not quite so selfishly casual in their life-styles as they liked to boast. Or perhaps it was because they could not accept that their parents might have known about back doors...

Andrew spoke more quickly. 'There's a complete alarm system downstairs, but parts of it can be isolated. So I switch off when I leave and then the door's locked and bolted and the alarm switched on again.'

'A carefully worked-out routine.'

'Kind of ... Only last night something went wrong. I left the house, crossed the courtyard and stepped out through the gateway and then saw—leastwise I thought I saw—something move.' He stopped jingling the coins. 'So I switched on my torch and there was this man. The next thing was, he belted me on the head and I was in cloud-land. Who the hell could he have been? Someone intending to break into the house?'

'That's the obvious answer. And you turned up suddenly, scaring him white-haired. Can you describe him? He might be one of our regulars.'

'He looked like he'd been in a fight, or something; his face was bloody.'

'Let's get specific. Was he tall, dark, and handsome, or short, fair, and ugly?'

'I didn't have time for all that. All I had was a pencil torch and everything happened so quickly.'

'You may have noticed more than you think, so we'll do a check-list. Was his hair straight or curly, cut old-fashioned back and sides or modern Mohawk? High forehead or low one? Intelligent-looking or a bit of a moron? Face

36

oval, round, oblate...'

'I keep telling you, I didn't catch any of that.'

'Very well. What was he wearing?'

'A suit.'

'A what?'

'A suit, Dad. You know, squares wear them.'

Stone rubbed his chin. 'That's a new one on me.'

'I'm not making it up.'

'I'm not trying to suggest you are; merely stating that in over twenty years in the force, I've never before heard of a man putting on a suit before making a break-in. Still, it adds tone to the neighbourhood.'

Andrew remained stony-faced.

'So what happened when you came to?'

'I felt like the top of my head had been blown off.'

'And after you discovered it hadn't been?'

'Well, I remembered you saying that if someone broke into a house, he'd leave a window or door open so as he could make a quick exit and I checked to see if any was, but the house was completely locked up. I reckoned he'd cleared off.'

'Far and away the most likely thing. You didn't hear a car start up?'

'There wasn't anything.'

'Took off while you were still unconscious ... Why didn't you tell us when you got back that you'd been injured?'

'I ... Well, I ...'

'Reluctant to go into explanations in front of your mother? Let me see the damage.' Andrew came down the greenhouse and Stone examined the walnut-sized bump and heavy bruising. 'Nasty, but it doesn't look life-threatening ... Have you been sick or seen double?'

'No.'

'No problems in moving; no lack of co-ordination?'

'Nothing except this bloody awful head.'

'At the first sign of anything else, it's straight to the doctor, even if that does mean admitting to your mother that you didn't spend the night singing psalms.'

'Dad ...'

'Well?'

'I don't know what to do about all this?'

'That's obvious. First, report it to the police, explaining why ...'

'But ...'

'Let me finish. Explaining why the delay. Two, tell Mr Ogilvy. The last being something you'd even more rather not do because it'll make it obvious that your departure from the house was both late and unorthodox, and it's my guess he didn't even know he was entertaining you in the first case.'

'It's not funny.'

'I'm not laughing. You could have been very seriously injured ...' Stone scratched his forehead, just below the point where the brown, curly hair was beginning to recede to leave a widow's peak. Surely there were times when a man had the right to be a father before he was a policeman? 'I imagine you phoned this morning to find out from Joanna if anything unusual happened after your departure?'

'She wasn't in.'

'Who did you speak to—one of the servants?'

'It's the couples' holiday, which is why ... I spoke to Mr Ogilvy. He just said Joanna wasn't at home.'

'So there's no real help there, despite the negative lack of any comment from him ... Do you, or don't you, tell? I'd say the answer to that has to rest on whether, despite the evidence there is to the contrary, the house was in fact burgled. If it was, your evidence, however meagre, could be important and that means it must be given. If it wasn't, should you still tell Ogilvy because of the possibility that the man might return? It sounds as if the house is already as well protected as is practicable. In addition to which, it is a fact that most villains are irrationally superstitious and if they think a proposed job has bad vibes, they'll not touch it, however attractive it otherwise is. Your assailant will have believed you to be another would-be breaker and to run into you outside the intended mark will have created vibes so

39

bad that he almost certainly won't go near the place again, even if he's told the Crown Jewels are there. All of which suggests that the best thing is for me to find out if any break-in has been reported.'

'You'll do that, Dad?'

'On the understanding that if it turns out there was one, you'll admit the truth both to the police and to Mr Ogilvy.'

'Thanks a million.'

'I'll require help. You must hold your mother's attention while I make the telephone call—if she hears me talking about Elsett Court, she'll smell a rat.'

They left the greenhouse and crossed to the kitchen, where June was cooking. Andrew engaged her in conversation while Stone went through to the hall. The telephone was on a small table by the clumsy mahogany coat-stand—a family heirloom which June, ever sentimental, had not yet found the will to discard. He dialled divisional HQ and spoke to the duty detective-constable. 'Mike, has there been any report of a break-in at Elsett Court?'

'Hang on and I'll check for sure, but I'm pretty certain there hasn't.' The wait was brief. 'Nothing, Sarge. Have you heard something, then?'

'Just a whisper which I thought was probably false.'

'Listening to whispers on your day off?'

'An overwhelming sense of duty.'

The DC's final comment was short, but sharp.

Stone returned to the kitchen and as June's back was to him, gave Andrew the thumbs-up sign. 'Who's for a drink? There's bitter, lager, Martini, gin, or sherry.'

'If that's the sherry Uncle Robin gave us, it's only good for cooking. He's a dear, but his taste in sherries is terrible.' She stirred the contents of a saucepan with a wooden spoon. 'I think I'd like a Martini with a dash of soda, please.'

Stone said to Andrew: 'And you?'

'Nothing, thanks.'

'I should think not!' June's voice was sharp.

Stone, amused that circumstances made it preferable to leave her thinking Andrew was suffering from a hangover, went through to the larder, where the drinks were kept. When he returned with two glasses, Andrew said: 'Dad, could I borrow the car tonight?'

'We're not doing anything, are we?' Stone asked June, as he handed her a glass.

She put the glass down by the side of the stove, stirred a little more quickly. 'Is something wrong with the bike?'

'No,' replied Andrew, 'but Joanna and I have been invited to a pretty smooth party and I can't ask her to ride pillion.'

'Doesn't she have that flashy sports car any longer?'

'For Pete's sake, woman,' Stone said, with

mock impatience, 'don't you know that when a man takes a lady to a party, he needs to be in the driving seat?'

Her lips tightened. Almost every emotion was spelled out on her round, full face, with wide, dark brown, vulnerable eyes.

CHAPTER FIVE

Andrew had learned from his father that a man's worth was not to be measured by his possessions, so he suffered no sense of inferiority when he drove up to Elsett Court in the family's four-year-old Escort. Ogilvy might run a Bentley and a Volvo estate, but that just made him lucky.

The gravel drive ended in a turning circle, in the centre of which was a raised flowerbed that for most of the year was, thanks to the skill of the gardener, filled with colour. Andrew switched off the engine and lights, climbed out of the Escort and crossed to the large, slightly pretentious porch. He rang the bell. The overhead light was switched on and the heavy, studded wooden door was opened by Ogilvy. Tall, well built, his face was long and smoothly handsome, despite the high-set eyes and very square chin. Exercise kept him in good physical shape.

'Good evening, Mr Ogilvy.' Andrew was not

intimidated by Ogilvy as a man; he was by Ogilvy as a father.

'Evening.' Ogilvy's politeness normally had a touch of glacier about it.

'Is Joanna ready?'

'How do you mean?'

'Is she ready to go to the party?'

'Didn't you understand when you phoned this morning that she wouldn't be going to it because she wouldn't be here?'

'I thought you were saying she was just out shopping.'

'I should have made myself clearer. The fact is, though, I was so certain she would have been in touch with you ... You'd better come in instead of standing out there. And perhaps you'd like a drink?'

Andrew followed Ogilvy into the green sitting-room—no longer furnished in green— much the smaller of the two and used when the family were on their own. Over the marble mantelpiece hung a portrait of Diana Ogilvy, painted the year before her death. Joanna closely resembled her in looks—light brown, wavy hair, blue eyes, neat nose, and wide sensuous mouth—but the painting suggested that she had been as neat in person and mind as Joanna was careless.

'What would you like?' Ogilvy asked. 'I can offer you virtually anything.'

Hoping to prove him wrong, Andrew chose a Malibu; it was a vain hope.

43

Having served the drinks, Ogilvy stood in front of the large fireplace, a balloon glass in the palm of his left hand. Andrew drank, said: 'Has Joanna gone away somewhere?'

'Betty rang this morning and said she was in the middle of some emotional crisis—the young lady over-indulges in them—and had to get away from everything and begged Joanna to go with her as support. Probably unwisely, Joanna agreed. She packed a suitcase and left, not very long before you phoned ... Have you met Betty?'

'No, I haven't.'

'An amusing young lady when not in crisis. Quite unlike her mother who would never suffer an emotional anything.'

'Do you know where they were going?'

'Initially, possibly to Betty's place in Shropshire, but after that the plan was to continue north to the Highlands. I gather that the idea is Betty should renew her soul among the freedom of isolation—but that may just have been Joanna's making fun of her.'

'And before she left, Joanna never said anything about the Burrows' party?'

'I had no idea there was to be one.'

'I wonder why on earth...' Andrew came to a stop, realizing he was in danger of betraying how bitter was his disappointment because the worm of jealousy had reared its head...

'She certainly should have let you know before she left, even if Betty tends to

44

anaesthetize one's mind. They're possibly spending the night at her home, so why not ring and find out?'

'I don't think I'll bother. Thanks all the same.' Andrew hoped he sounded sufficiently laid back to project the image of a man sophisticated enough to view a woman's unthinking behaviour with amusement rather than resentment.

'And remind her,' continued Ogilvy, as if Andrew had not spoken, 'that the eighth circle of hell is reserved for seducers, sorcerers, thieves, hypocrites, and those who forget appointments ... Use the phone in the library.'

As he followed Ogilvy through the hall and into the library, which contained enough leather-bound books to nurture the most thirsty of minds, Andrew nervously wondered if seducers had been in the original?

Ogilvy crossed to the far side of a large partners' desk, pulled open a drawer, brought out a small black book and flicked through the pages, stopped when he found the one he wanted. He dialled a number, handed the receiver to Andrew, left the room and carefully closed the door behind himself.

As he listened to the ringing sound, Andrew wondered whether Joanna's decision had been quite so casually reached as her father made out—Betty might so easily have a brother. And what in the hell was he going to say? Joanna hated anyone's trying to 'corral' her and she demanded the right to live without explanations. If he bluntly asked why she'd gone away with Betty when they'd a date that evening, she'd reply that it was because she'd wanted to and would slam down the receiver; if he asked whether Betty had a brother, she'd laugh before she slammed down the receiver. He had to approach sideways. Ask if she'd had a good journey up ... There was no answer; no chance to approach sideways or head on.

Back in the green room, he said: 'There was no reply.'

Ogilvy was seated in one of the chairs. 'Then I expect the rest of the family are out at some social event, of which there seem to be a plenitude, and they've decided to head for the hills right away. One hopes for Joanna's sake that the renewal of Betty's soul proceeds smoothly and does not occasion another emotional crisis.' He stood. 'Let me get you a refill.'

'I won't, thanks. Not with having to drive back home.'

'Very commendable.'

That, thought Andrew, could just as easily have been an expression of ironic amusement as genuine approbation. Ogilvy's manner was too smooth to be able to judge which.

'Is your father very busy at the moment?'

He'd been about to leave; now, social manners demanded that he did not do so immediately. 'He is, rather.'

'In a recession, I suppose crime investigation is the one job in which there's no need to fear redundancy. I read the other day that crime was necessary if honesty was to be defined. Would you think that that could be right?'

'No. A policeman doesn't have to be sliced up with a broken bottle to prove it's wrong to injure someone.'

'How right you are! And how good to hear a robust, practical answer from an undergraduate and not a wishywashy, pseudo-intellectual one.'

Ogilvy was normally so coldly distant in manner that Andrew found a disturbing quality in his present friendliness. Betty's brother became more real. Almost certainly, little would please Ogilvy more than to see Joanna becoming very friendly with someone from her own background...

'If your father's busy, I take it there's a lot of crime in the district?'

'No more than in every division.'

'Nothing special going on at the moment?'

'I don't think so, no.'

A carriage clock struck the half-hour and immediately, so that it seemed to become a false echo, so did the longcase in the hall. 'I'd better get moving,' Andrew said.

'If Joanna rings me—and being a modern miss, I suppose that's rather unlikely—I'll tell her she has to make her abject apologies to you.'

He knew damn well that Joanna would never make an abject apology to anyone, Andrew thought bitterly. 'Thanks for the drink.'

Ogilvy accompanied Andrew to the front door and when he said goodbye, added the rider that he hoped they'd soon have the chance to have another interesting conversation.

'Bastard,' said Andrew as he settled behind the wheel of the Escort, referring not to Ogilvy, but to the brother of Betty who now stood tall, handsome, and at the very least the heir to an estate.

He drove off, accelerating too harshly so that the front tyres scrabbled on the loose gravel. When Joanna returned, he'd not rush to get in touch with her; he'd leave her to make the going ... If only he didn't know he was lying to himself. The moment she was back, he'd be rushing...

There were two possible routes to Peteringham; the more direct one which was the slower, since it lay through country lanes, and the two-sides-of-a-triangle one which made use of the London road. He chose to take the former. It was at the first crossroads that a car drew up behind the Escort, forcing him to depress the rear-view mirror to its anti-dazzle position.

A small van, coming down the hill from his right, passed and the road was clear. He drove

48

across and continued along the lane, bordered by thorn hedges, to reach a T-junction, where he turned right. Irritatingly, the following car remained too close for comfort, yet did not pull out to pass. He reached a second crossroads at which, so tradition said, a gibbet had once been erected and, satisfied the way was clear, drove over. The car behind closed until the interior of the Escort was so sharply illuminated that reflections off bright surfaces distracted him. Determined to make the other car pass him, he braked to little more than a walking speed.

The car finally did pass, but then it cut across the Escort's bows to force Andrew to brake to a stop so sharply that he came hard up against the seat-belt. 'You're bloody mad,' he shouted in exasperation.

Two men jumped out of the back of the car and raced across; as they came within the glare of the headlights, he knew a sudden frightening sense of panicky disorientation because it seemed as if they had Mickey Mouse faces.

The driving door was wrenched open, the point of a knife put to his throat. 'Get over to the passenger seat.'

He was too shocked to move.

The second man, who'd climbed into the back of the Escort, grabbed him by the hair and wrenched; the pain reached through his bewilderment and forced him to scramble across to the front passenger seat. The knife was once again put to his throat. The first man settled behind the wheel, twice flicked the headlights up to full beam and then back. The car ahead drove off and they followed it.

At the mill—now no more than a store for a major animal food distributor—they turned right into a lane which, a mile further on, ended at a ragstone quarry, abandoned many years previously. They stopped by a tumbledown shed.

The driver of the Escort got out, walked around the bonnet, pulled open the door and shone a torch on Andrew's face. The man in the back reached over Andrew's right shoulder and there was an uncapped bottle in his hand. 'Start drinking.'

'But...'

The bottle was thrust so hard against his mouth that he had to open his lips and teeth. What he identified as whisky poured into his mouth, causing him to choke and cough violently, spraying the windscreen.

'Drink or we slice your bleeding throat.'

He drank. After several mouthfuls, he stopped, pulled his head back.

'All of it.'

'But I can't take any more...'

His nose was pinched, making him open his mouth. He drank, gagged, drank. His stomach churned as his senses began to play him false, removing the sharp edge of fear and replacing this with a sense of disengagement...

The world began to spin away, making him

dizzy, and waves of nausea swept his stomach. He mumbled that he had to get out of the car and tried to move, but once again the man in the back seat grabbed his hair to hold him fast. He fought the nausea as long as he could, but then vomited wildly. Not very much later, he blacked out.

CHAPTER SIX

The alarm woke Stone. He turned on to his back and stared up at the ceiling, weakly allowing himself another minute or two before he got up.

'Did you hear Andy come back?' June asked.

'Can't say I did.'

'I thought I heard the car, but as no one came upstairs, it can't have been him.'

He yawned.

'He must come home at a reasonable hour.'

'Love, we went through all this yesterday. And you know there was a party. If he follows the milkman, that's up to him.'

'No, it isn't. You need the car.'

'Joe's passing by and picking me up. Which by the same token means that I'd better get a move on.' He threw back the bedclothes, climbed out of bed and hurried through to the bathroom.

When he returned, she said: 'I wish you'd worry a bit more about him.'

'And I wish you'd worry a bit less.'

'Sometimes I wonder if you really care about him.'

'That's just being plain daft.' He went round to her side of the bed, bent down and kissed her. 'Don't you know that, for me, he sits at your right hand.'

'That ... that's blasphemous.'

He chuckled, kissed her again, straightened up. 'I'll see you when I see you.'

'Don't let them go on and on overworking you.'

'You know the Guv'nor—every week has eight days, every day has twenty-five hours.'

'And who's the first to moan about that? Marie.'

It was the first time he'd heard that she complained about the hours her husband worked. A pity her complaints didn't bear more fruit!

He went downstairs. When June had been younger—before Andrew had been born—and he'd had an early start, she'd insisted on getting up and cooking him breakfast before he left. Since then, he'd persuaded her to stay in bed until a more reasonable time. He was certain she suffered a conscience when she did.

Sandwiches, in clingfilm, were in the refrigerator. He collected them before he left by the kitchen door. As he walked to the passage which went up the side of the house, he checked that everything was as it should be in his own and his neighbour's garden. It was said that one could always identify a man who was either a policeman or a crook—he was forever looking about himself.

When he reached the end of the passage, it was to find that the Escort was parked on what had originally been the front garden, but was now surfaced. He smiled. So much for June's boast that she always heard her son! Obviously, Andrew had slipped into the house without her hearing a sound.

It was only when he was abreast of the car that he realized Andrew lay slumped across the front seats. Arrived home so late that he'd decided it would cause less hassle to sleep out the rest of the night in the car. Stone opened the nearside door, intending to wake Andrew and suggest he made for bed, was met by the acrid stench of stale whisky and vomit.

His first reaction was one of anger; his second, fear. Andrew must have been so drunk that only fool's luck had enabled him to reach home. Goddammit, he silently shouted, could the young never learn? He reached in and grabbed Andrew's shoulder and shook, but gained as much reaction as if he had been handling a sack of potatoes.

He heard an approaching car slow down and, since traffic was light this early in the morning, could be reasonably certain that this was Joe Masefield. Masefield was not a man with whom to share confidences. If he learned Andrew had been so plastered that on reaching home he had collapsed in the car, he'd happily, and without the slightest ill-will, pass the news on that boys would be boys. Stone slammed the door of the Escort shut and carried on through the opened gateway to the pavement.

The nearly new Astra—Masefield knew nothing about saving money—drew up and Stone climbed in.

'You're lucky I'm here because did I have a night of it! Went down to the Dirty Duck for a pint or two and ran into a sharp little number with eyes that didn't just say bed, they turned the bedclothes down...'

Stone could never make up his mind whether Masefield was a fluent liar, lived his off-duty hours in a world of fantasy, or could have offered Don Juan a few useful tips.

* * *

Kemp, the detective-inspector, was a man easy to admire but difficult to like. He had the lean and hungry look of the ambitious man, the drive and determination to bring that ambition to fruition. He accepted men's failings, but found most difficult to understand and impossible to condone. For him, both right and wrong could be sharply defined.

He looked up. His black hair was cut short

and very well brushed, his nose was aggressive, and when he smiled—there were some who would have said if—he always seemed to do so with reservations. 'Is there anything in the night's reports?'

That, translated, meant was there anything of sufficient importance to need his immediate attention.

'I don't think so, sir,' Stone replied, as he stood in front of the desk. 'A handful of minor break-ins, a couple of domestics, an affray at one of the pubs with minor injuries, a hit-and-run—we're waiting to hear from the hospital as to the victim's condition—and Maggie, ever hopeful.'

'What are you talking about?'

Stone wondered if Kemp were quite as humourless away from work. 'Old Margaret Crundle, sir. Almost every week, she claims to have been raped. We've had a word with various services to see if there's something can be done for her, but it appears that, ignoring the rape claims, she's sufficiently sane to be able to dictate her own life.' He waited for further comment, but there was none. He passed the night's crime list across the desk.

The DI put the list down without bothering to read it, accepting Stone's judgement that all the cases were routine. 'About the Chandler case...'

Twenty minutes later, Stone left and went down the corridor to the CID general room where he checked with the DCs how work in hand was progressing and allocating the investigations into the previous night's crimes.

Back in his own room and seated, he stared at the small, framed photograph of June and Andrew on the right-hand side of the desk. How was June going to react to finding Andrew had drunk himself hoggishly incapable? Normally reluctant to create any kind of a scene, if someone or something threatened the family unit, she turned into a virago. She had learned from him how rarely were the tragic consequences of drunken driving confined either in time or person to those immediately involved. And with her overactive imagination, she would have 'seen' the accident Andrew might have had, would have been at his side as he lay in the intensive-care unit, hovering between life and death. And 'experiencing' the anguish of these scenes, she surely would have told Andrew what she thought of his behaviour in terms that a Grimsby fishwife might envy ... Her reactions, since they would have been so alien to her nature, must have shaken Andrew far more thoroughly than any condemnation from him could manage...

His thoughts were interrupted by a phone call from Peteringham General Hospital. A woman with a falsely pitched voice said that Steve Hutton had had an emergency operation, but despite this his condition had deteriorated and was now critical. No prognosis could be given.

Clearly, Hutton might die as a direct consequence of the hit-and-run and therefore it had been a mistake not to single out the case earlier when reporting on the night's crimes. Where the DI was concerned, it was far better to admit a mistake as soon as it was recognized rather than hope that such admission would not have to be made, only to discover that it did. Stone shuffled through the reports in order to refresh his mind before reporting to Kemp.

There were two witnesses. The PC who'd taken the first statement had added the letters ABD, meaning Eastwick was a little bit doddery. The grey car had hit the motorcyclist as it overtook. He couldn't identify the make of car and hadn't tried to take the number. The second witness, Ormond, had just turned into Westbreak Road when a car, weaving badly, passed him at speed. It was a fawn hatchback, possibly an Escort. The initial letter of the registration was probably E; he didn't get the numbers; the last three letters were RKO—he could be quite certain of them because they were the initials of his wife. There had been no oncoming traffic and should have been more than enough room to overtake in perfect safety. After the accident, the car had speeded up and driven off, disappearing right at the T-junction.

The police called to the scene had, after the

departure of the ambulance, carried out standard routine. They had found slivers of glass which, since the motorbike's lights were intact, had probably come from the car's lights. The bike was now with Vehicles.

Stone stood, metaphorically squared his shoulders. Forward to the DI...

*   *   *

As detective-sergeant, he didn't work shifts, but that didn't mean he enjoyed shorter days. It was after seven in the evening before he arrived home. He'd only just shut the front door when June hurried out of the sitting-room. 'Did you see Andy this morning before you left?'

He hung up his mackintosh. 'Yes.'

'Then why on earth didn't you do something?'

'Joe turned up almost at once.'

'But he was in a disgusting state.' Her voice was shrill. 'How could you have left him like that?'

'Come on through and I'll try to explain.' He put his arm around her, but she shrugged it aside and hurried into the sitting-room.

She sat while he stood by the overfilled bookcase which bore witness to their love of reading. The carpet had been turned end to end to hide a worn patch, the three-piece suite was becoming frayed, and the curtains were faded

58

about the leading edges. A room that might have looked a trifle dowdy, but didn't. Perhaps this was because in some way it reflected the fact that with their priorities, if Andrew needed financial help to pursue his studies, which he did—he received a grant, but this was no more sufficient than for any other undergraduate— they viewed the worn carpet, frayed furniture, and faded curtains with a sense of pride rather than shame.

She stared angrily at her husband. 'Don't you know that people die from being drunk and left alone?'

'They die because they choke on their own vomit. Since Andy had so obviously brought up everything, I didn't reckon there was any risk of that.'

'But...'

'Listen. When I realized Andy was there, I could hear Joe's car. If Joe had seen him in that state, the news would have been around the station at the speed of light. Surely we didn't want the world to know that Andy had made a grisly spectacle of himself?'

She brushed a stray hair back from her high forehead.

'If there'd been any risk to him, I'd have sent Joe on his way and then done something.'

'I ... I suppose you could be right.'

'How is he now?'

'It took me ages to rouse him and then I had to help him up to his room. An hour ago I went up to see if he wanted anything and the mention of food seemed to panic him.'

'He'll be at the stage where he's sworn to become a lifelong teetotaller.'

'In God's name, why did he drink like that? Especially when he knew he had to drive home.'

'I've no answer. Still, with any luck he'll have learned a lesson.'

'Is that all you've got to say?'

'If you mean, am I going to read him the Riot Act—haven't you already told him what you think?'

'Of course I have.'

'Then any comments of mine will come as an anticlimax.'

She refused to respond to his lighter approach. 'You must make him realize how stupid he's been.'

'If you think that's necessary.'

'It's all Joanna's fault.'

'He's only the one person to blame, himself.'

'She'll have egged him on.'

'Is that what he claims?'

'He hasn't said anything, but it's obvious.'

'I wonder? I'd have said that she's sufficiently level-headed in this sort of thing to try to stop him boozing rather than egging him on.'

'You just can't see beyond the pretty face and understand how much she'd enjoy watching him make a fool of himself.'

'I doubt that very much.'

She was silent for a moment, then said: 'I've cleaned the car up as well as I could, but haven't really got rid of the smell, so I've left all the windows open.'

'Will it help if I give it a second go?'

'Almost certainly.'

'Then give me what I need and I'll get cracking.'

She took a deep breath, then said with a rush: 'It could have been so terrible. I mean, even as it was he hit something but, thank God, didn't injure himself.'

'How d'you know he did?'

'One of the headlamps is broken.'

His voice was suddenly harsh. 'Which one?'

Startled, she said nervously: 'I can't remember. What does it matter?'

'I just wondered,' he answered, trying to speak more calmly so that his voice did not continue to betray his sudden fear.

'The car's quite all right except for that. It won't cost much to replace, will it?'

'I shouldn't think so.'

'I'm sure it won't. Shall I give you the cleaning things, then? The sooner it's done, the better.'

They went through to the kitchen where she half-filled a bucket with warm water, to which she added a measure of detergent, and searched under the sink for a plastic sponge. 'The trouble is, the mess got down into the corners which are so difficult to get at.'

'I'll do what I can.'

'Tomorrow, when it's dry, perhaps we could spray with something like lavender water.'

'And have everyone believe we're just back from a Turkish brothel.'

She was too worried to respond to his facetious comment.

He left the kitchen and went round the outside of the house to the front. The Escort was facing inwards, which explained why he'd noticed nothing when he'd returned earlier, and he came to a stop, put down the bucket, studied the nearside headlamp with its shattered glass. An overtaking car would have struck the motorcyclist with the nearside...

When he'd read the report of the hit-and-run, it had not begun to occur to him that Andrew could be involved, even though he'd known Andrew had been drunk, the car involved was probably a fawn hatchback, possibly an Escort, and the registration letters were RKO and probably E. Disasters only happened to other families ... Despite the coincidences, this surely had to be ridiculous? Andrew had been at a party with Joanna, not driving drunkenly through one of the less salubrious parts of Peteringham...

CHAPTER SEVEN

As Stone stepped into the hall and closed the door, June came through from the kitchen. 'D'you need something more?'

He couldn't make sense of her question because his mind was elsewhere and racing. 'What?'

'Gerry, is something wrong? Why are you looking like that?'

If he answered her truthfully, she'd become frantically worried. And it wouldn't do any good to try and explain that even while he accepted the absurdity of his fears, nevertheless he had to make certain they really were absurd. 'I've decided before I start work to look in on Andy and see if he's up to giving a hand.'

'That's a good idea. It'll make him understand what a beastly mess he made … But don't force him if he's really not up to it.'

He climbed the stairs and went into the end bedroom. Andrew, curled up in bed, faced the door and there was sufficient light coming through the curtains to mark the signs of suffering on his face. 'I want a word.'

'Not now, Dad.'

Stone crossed to the window and pulled back the curtains. The day was sunny, with only a few puffballs of cloud, and sunlight streamed into the room. 'Sit up.'

'Jesus, Dad! I feel ghastly.'

'However near to death, you'll sit up and tell me what happened last night.' There was a chair, in front of the table on which was a BBC computer and printer, and he set it by the side of the bed, sat.

Andrew slowly struggled into a sitting position.

'Did you go to Joanna's place last night?'

'What's it matter?'

'Did you?'

'Yes,' he muttered sullenly.

'Where was the party, when did you arrive there, when did you leave?'

'She wasn't there.'

'Does that mean you didn't go to the party?'

'It wouldn't have been much bloody fun on my own.' He noticed his father's expression, hastily adopted a more conciliatory tone. 'It's like they were all going to be Joanna's friends and I wouldn't have known more'n a couple of 'em. And some of her crowd keep their noses a long way above the horizontal.'

'So what did you do?'

'I...' He came to a stop.

'You what?'

'Does it matter?'

'It matters one hell of a lot.'

'But I can't see ... All right, all right. After a bit of a chat with her dad, I left and ...' He was silent for a while, then said in a rush: 'Can one's mind suddenly flip?'

It was so unexpected a question that it left Stone momentarily bewildered. 'Why d'you ask?'

'Because ... Well, because of what happened. Dad, you've got to believe me.'

'Why should I find that difficult?'

Andrew mumbled something, climbed out of bed, groaning as he did so, and hurriedly left. Stone stared at nothing and tried not to believe that his fears were going to be justified.

When Andrew returned, he silently climbed into bed, lay back with closed eyes.

'What happened on your drive home?'

'I ... I decided to return the back way. At the first crossroads a car came right up my exhaust pipe and stayed there and wouldn't go past. In the end, I slowed down to make it go by, but when it did it cut across and made me stop. Two men got out of it and they were wearing ...' He came to a stop.

'Masks and they forced you to drink yourself into a stupor.'

'How d'you know that?'

'I've been in the force long enough to have heard every conceivable excuse for becoming blind drunk.'

'I swear that's the truth. They were wearing Mickey Mouse masks.'

'The truth? Joanna wasn't in, which pissed you off so much you went on a pub crawl and ended up so plastered you've no idea what

65

happened.'

'Why won't you believe me?'

'Because you're proving short on imagination. You're forgetting that the impossible is more readily accepted than the unlikely. So next time, introduce little green men from Mars with turnip ears.'

'Bloody humorous!'

'No. Bloody tragic.'

'You're so pompous about the law that you're just preprogrammed. Only a rotter gets tight. I was tight, therefore I'm a rotter. Never, ever believe a rotter.'

'Last night, just before eleven, a lad of your age, riding a motorbike, was mown down by a hit-and-run car. He's still alive, but only just. The odds have to be that the driver of the car was tight.'

'It happens.'

'The car was probably a light fawn Escort and the registration letters were RKO and probably E.'

It took several seconds for the inference to sink into Andrew's befuddled mind. 'Christ, it wasn't me.'

'How can you be certain? You can't remember anything after you were forced to drink yourself stupid.'

'I'd know if something like that had happened.'

Stone stood.

Andrew stared up, a pleading expression on

his face. 'It couldn't have been me.'

Stone left and went downstairs, to find June was waiting in the hall. 'Why's Andy shouting?' she asked.

'He was trying to convince me of something.'

'Convince you of what?'

He went past her and through the kitchen to the larder where he poured out two whiskies. She watched him from the doorway, terrified by his silence. When he came out of the larder and handed her a glass, she said in a whisper: 'Please tell me.' Her large brown eyes were filled with panic.

'Joanna wasn't at home. That left him frustrated and angry and so he went boozing, ending up plastered. Naturally, though, he has a different version. He was driving back here when he was carved up by another car. Two men in Mickey Mouse masks got out and forced him to drink himself unconscious.'

'Men in Mickey Mouse masks?'

'I told him that shows a lack of imagination.'

'But ... It's got to be that he's ashamed and rather stupidly trying to make out he's not responsible...'

'If only it were that simple. Last night, a lad was knocked off his motorbike in Westbreak Road and very severely injured; it's a lottery whether he lives or dies.'

'But you can't be suggesting that Andy had anything to do with that!'

'An eye-witness report names a fawn Escort with our registration letters; broken glass was found in the road and our car has a broken nearside headlamp.'

She made a sound that was both a cry of despair and of disbelief. Then she said, again expressing this contradiction: 'If he was so drunk he was unconscious, he couldn't have been driving.'

'Who else would have been?'

'Why won't you believe what he says?'

'Because I'm a sceptic when it comes to Mickey Mouse masks making someone drink himself into the ground.'

'He is your son.'

'Which means he's involved us.'

'What are you going to do?'

'I have no option.'

'You ... You're not saying you'll tell the police?'

'I am the police.'

'You're also his father. That means you ought to believe him, yet all you seem able to do is call him a liar.'

'The facts are that ...'

'He's told you what the facts are.' Her voice was shrill.

'If I could believe him ...'

'If you were a proper father, you would, no matter what.'

'That's being illogical.'

'Am I supposed to worry about being logical

when my husband says my son ... I suppose you'll only be satisfied when he's in jail?' She began to sob and tears trickled down her cheeks. She put her glass down on the table, ran out. A moment later he heard the slam of their bedroom door.

He drank quickly. What could he do if convinced of Andrew's guilt other than inform the DI of what he knew? Yet such an action on his part, which would upset any mother, could easily induce a mental breakdown in June...

Some of her first memories were of rows between her parents in which she had been blamed as the cause of all the troubles; only much later had she understood that because her birth had been so difficult, both physically and mentally, all sexual activity between her parents had ceased.

She could still recall in great detail the day when her father had left home to live with another woman. Her mother had been so hysterical that she had been convinced they'd been abandoned to die of hunger...

She had married at eighteen, desperately hoping to find the security that a loving husband could give her. The world usually being bloody-minded, her husband had turned out to be a bully, determined to dominate her. Part of his campaign had consisted of boasting of amorous conquests so numerous and in nature so perverse that had she not been already mentally scarred she must have recognized them to be the lies of an inadequate man. She'd become so convinced of her own unworthiness that when he'd been killed in a car crash, she had seen this as one more proof that she was accursed rather than a sign that fate had not completely forsaken her.

For two years she had lived the life of a zombie. Then she'd met a young PC who'd been very helpful when she had had her handbag snatched; so helpful that he had repeatedly visited her digs in order to check various facts...

Their married life had been marred only by the fact that she had wanted two children, but nature had decreed otherwise. Inevitably, they had had rows, but because he understood how she needed to know she was wanted, these had never threatened their relationship. Twenty years of happiness had built a shell which protected her from the horrors of her childhood and the humiliations of her first marriage, but it was a fragile shell. If he reported the facts of the hit-and-run as he now knew them to Kemp, he would surely shatter that shell. Yet if he kept silent, he would betray himself.

He poured a second, stronger whisky.

*   *   *

He was in the sitting-room when she came downstairs. She held her chin high and when

70

she looked at him her eyes were challenging. 'I've had a long talk with Andy.' She went over to the chair in which she usually sat. 'He's telling the truth and is absolutely positive that there's no way in which he could have driven the car after he'd been made to drink.'

'Then how did it get back here?'

'He's no idea.'

'The only possible alternative is that one of the men drove it.'

'Then that's what happened.'

'Why should anyone do such a thing?'

'How could I know?'

'Love, can't you understand how impossible all that is when...'

'He was forced to drink until he was unconscious. He could not have driven anywhere.'

She had armoured herself with a certainty that was beyond argument; a faith beyond logic. Yet this must make it all the more traumatic when eventually she was forced to face the truth...

'What are you going to do?' She suddenly stood, crossed the carpet, and knelt in front of him. 'Please, I beg you, believe him.'

CHAPTER EIGHT

Stone's room on the fourth floor of the ten-storey building was smaller than the DI's—as befitted his lower rank—but the view from the single window was the same; across the road was the William and Mary vicarage, with a large garden bordered by yew hedges, and behind, the fourteenth-century church, built of ragstone, noted for its fifteenth-century stained glass. It was a scene of peaceful continuity. Yet, he thought, repeatedly life proved that for an individual there was little peaceful continuity...

He turned, crossed to the desk, sat, dialled county HQ and asked for Vehicles. Had they anything on the motorbike in the Hutton hit-and-run?

'You think we've nothing to do but spoonfeed your division? Right now, we've four cars, one van, and the remains of a lorry, all of which came in before your bike.'

'I just wondered if you could give me the details from the acceptance chit. Sorry to rush things, but it looks like the victim's going to buy it and we'll have a death by reckless driving or manslaughter.'

After a minute the duty sergeant said: 'The initial point of impact was almost certainly the offside handlebar. There's a smear of paint on the footrest which suggests that as the bike went over, it reared up and the footrest hit the side of the car.'

'Will there be enough paint for comparison tests?'

'At a guess, it'll be a borderline case.'

'What colour is the paint?'

'Light. That's all I can tell you.'

As he replaced the receiver, he wondered what he was going to do if he found a scratch low down on the nearside of the Escort...

*   *   *

That morning he'd come to work by bus, leaving the Escort because he feared to have it in the car park at the station. He returned home at lunch-time in one of the CID cars—when it came to making the obligatory entry in the car's log, he'd use one of the other cases in which he was involved...

He parked, walked up the pavement to his house, turned into the surfaced area in front of it. Conscious of the rising tension within himself, he visually checked the nearside of the Escort. He knew a surge of relief when he saw that the paintwork was undamaged. But being a careful man, he knelt in order to look at the paintwork from a different angle and in a different light just to confirm...

Low down on the rear door there was a short, fine scratch which had reached down to

73

the primer, but not bare metal ... A parked car was often scratched because other people were careless. This scratch could so easily have been caused by someone's opening the door of another car that was parked too close ... He checked his thoughts, annoyed that he could so readily blind himself to the facts. That scratch made it significantly more likely that the Escort had been the hit-and-run car.

He stood and turned towards the door, only then realized that June was standing in the doorway. She stepped aside to let him enter and closed the door. 'What were you looking at?'

'A scratch.'

'Why?'

He told her.

'That doesn't prove Andy was driving at the time.'

He said nothing.

'He wants to talk to you.'

'Good. I want to talk to him.'

'Gerry ... Please, please remember you're his father as well as a policeman.'

'What does that mean?'

'Don't automatically assume he's a liar.'

'I won't. Where is he?'

'In the sitting-room, watching the telly.'

He crossed to the door, saw that she was following him. 'It'll be best if I talk to him on my own.'

'My God!' she said bitterly. 'Even now you

74

won't forget that you're Detective-Sergeant Stone.'

'Because I goddamn well daren't.' He opened the door. Andrew looked more human, but still hard used. When he saw his father, his mouth tightened. Stone shut the door, waited. Then he said: 'D'you mind turning off?'

Andrew took a shade too long to comply.

Stone sat. 'There's something you need to know. Paint was found on the bike which almost certainly came from the hit-and-run car. I've checked and there's a new scratch on the rear door of the Escort. Taken in conjunction with the other evidence, that as near as damnit nails our car.'

'I've told you...'

'And now you're going to tell me again.'

'What the hell's the use? You don't believe a word I say. Mum said you've as good as called me a bloody liar.'

'If you're not lying, how do you explain the sequence of events?'

'I can't.'

'And neither can I, which is why I'm hoping you'll manage to remember something more which will offer a line to work on.'

'And if I can't?'

Stone ignored the question. 'Did anything at all unusual happen on the drive to Ogilvy's place?'

Andrew spoke sullenly, but soon that sullenness dropped away. He began to add details which he now recalled and by the time he came to the end, he sounded almost confident.

'Joanna hadn't been in touch to say she was going north and so wouldn't make the party?'

'Not a word.'

'I imagine it's not unusual for her suddenly to change her mind?'

'Sure. But she'd let me know. She's not the kind of selfish, insensitive person you and Mum think her.'

'Ogilvy seemed to know nothing about the party or that you were meant to be taking her to it?'

'He'd no idea why I'd turned up that late.'

'Not knowing that it's a habit of yours to be around much later?'

Andrew looked uneasily at his father, realized the question had been facetious, managed a brief smile.

'You can promise me you had only one drink with him?'

'I asked for a Malibu, sort of hoping he wouldn't have any. When he offered me another, I said no, thanks, I was driving.'

'It sounds as if he was quite friendly?'

'I've never known him so. I mean, usually he's about as welcoming as a block of ice.'

'When you drove off, would you say you were in full control of yourself?'

'All I'd had was that one Malibu.'

'Was there another car parked anywhere

near the house when you left?'

'If there was, I didn't see it.'

'This car that came up behind you—have you any idea what make or model it was?'

'No way, not with its headlights blinding me all the time we were moving. Then things happened too fast for me to worry.'

'Did it try to pass before you slowed right down?'

'It just kept up my exhaust pipe, making things difficult.'

'How were the two men in masks dressed?'

'I don't really know. I mean, when I first saw them I thought my brain must have flipped. When a knife was put to my throat, I didn't care what in the hell they were wearing.'

'Did they suggest why they should want to make you drunk?'

'They hardly spoke; when they did, it was to tell me what to do.'

'What's the last thing you can remember?'

'Feeling like I was spiralling down into a bottomless well.'

Stone stood, walked over to the window and stared out. 'Have you been into drugs of any sort?'

'You know I haven't.'

He turned. 'All I can be certain of is that you've never shown any of the usual signs.'

'You're admitting you've been keeping tabs on me because you reckon I'm a potential junkie?'

'These days, any caring father keeps an eye lifting because, tragically, a happy home has ceased to be a defence against addiction. And an addict can very soon find himself owing his supplier a small fortune which he cannot hope to repay. Then it's a toss-up whether the pusher draws him into doing some street pushing or calls some pals out to work him over as an example to others.'

'I've never so much as smoked a single joint.'

'Good ... So you've no idea why anyone should want to frame you?'

'There's no one. And I suppose that means I've got to be a liar?'

'It means things are going to be that much more difficult ... Do you know anyone who lives near Westbreak Road?'

'Where's that?'

'South-east Peteringham.'

'I don't know anyone from that part of town.'

'I reckon that's it, then; we've covered just about everything.'

'Big deal,' said Andrew, but sounded scared, not defiant.

*   *   *

Stone settled behind the wheel of the CID Renault and started the engine, but did not immediately drive off. He'd assured June that he'd been impressed by Andrew's evidence,

78

making it sound as if he now accepted all he'd been told. But that was an exaggeration, if not a lie. He didn't believe—but he didn't disbelieve as conclusively as before. Two things about Andrew's story had struck him. At no time had Andrew contradicted himself— even a practised liar found it difficult to remain consistent. By bringing up the subject of drugs, he'd offered Andrew a chance to suggest a motive, but that had been turned down—liars usually grabbed a chance to bolster their lies.

He finally drove off but at the second T-junction turned right, instead of left, to head away from divisional HQ.

South-east Peteringham was one of the poor parts of town; most of the houses were terraced, with no front gardens and only pocket-handkerchief-size back ones, built in late Victorian times to accommodate those who worked for the railway, building and repairing rolling stock. Ten years before the works had been closed and all the men made redundant; a large number of them had been too old to be retrained to other skills and the percentage of unemployed had remained consistently higher than in other areas.

There were four public houses reasonably near to Westbreak Road and he visited each in turn. He spoke to all those who worked there and showed them a family photograph with June and himself blanked off. Did he or she remember seeing this young man on Saturday night, probably around half-ten? No one did.

He left town and drove towards Sad's Cross, turning off at the mill and continuing up the lane to the abandoned quarry. There was a surrounding fence and gate, erected to keep out trespassers, but the fence had been breached in several places and the metal gate had collapsed and been shunted to one side so that there was room to drive through. He parked in front of a tumbledown shed and climbed out. A light breeze ruffled his curly hair as he studied the lie of the land. According to Andrew, the Escort had been parked near this shed. He began to search the ground which, too hard to take impressions, was littered with plastic bottles, beer and soft drink cans, wrapping paper ... The possibility of finding and identifying anything among all this rubbish that would support Andrew's story seemed so remote that even an optimist would not waste his time trying; detectives were trained to be neither optimists nor pessimists. He found half a walking stick and used that to poke around among the clumps of grass, weeds, brambles, thistles, and bracken. He was half way to the edge of the quarried area when he exposed an empty bottle of Haig with the label untarnished by weather. There had been no rain for five days, but before that there had been several days of intermittent or steady rain and if the bottle had been lying out for more than six then the label would probably have shown signs of weathering.

He returned to the Renault, unlocked the boot and opened up the scene-of-crime box. From that, he brought out a pair of disposable gloves and put these on. He picked up the bottle and, back at the car, dusted it with dark powder. There were no fingerprints, only smudges to indicate that whoever had last held it had been wearing gloves. How many people who came to a place like this wore gloves?

*   *   *

An army marched on its stomach; a police force stumbled on its paperwork. Stone was reading through the P16 form that had to accompany the RT5 form, and checking both against the original entry in the DC's notebook in order to certify there had been no omissions or alterations, when the door opened and Wearing entered. He was a tall, thin, morose-looking man who was popularly supposed to be a miser; even had that been true, he could surely have claimed his five children as cause enough.

'I've been on to the DVLC at Swansea, Sarge.'

'What about?'

Wearing was vaguely astonished by the question. 'The hit-and-run in Westbreak Road.'

Stone, hoping his expression had not

changed, looked up. 'And?'

'They moaned like hell, of course, but in the end agreed to draw up a list as soon as possible. They'll cover E and F years. Like I said to 'em, it's not everyone's eyes can tell the difference at a distance and in artificial light.'

'Who initiated the request?'

'The Guv'nor. Came into our room after lunch and said that as he couldn't find you, one of us was to deal with it.'

'Did Swansea give any indication of how long they'll take?'

'We'll be lucky to get the list before the weekend.'

'OK.'

Wearing nodded, went over to the door. 'Bad luck on the poor bastard, isn't it? They thought they were going to pull him through, but now it doesn't seem there's much hope,' he said as he left.

Stone should have phoned the hospital that morning to find out how Steven Hutton was. At the training college the instructors had repeatedly emphasized that a policeman who allowed his personal emotions to interfere with his professional duties was a poor policeman. By that token, he thought, he'd become a goddamn awful one.

He fiddled with the pencil. Swansea had been asked to draw up a list of owners of cars whose registration letters were RKO and whose year letter was E or F. When that list came through, various possibilities would be provisionally eliminated—luxury-sized cars, colours which could hardly be confused with grey or fawn even in streetlighting, and owners who lived outside the county (obviously, the driver might be from out-of-county, but statistics showed that up to eighty-three per cent of accidents off the motorways involved vehicles which were owned by persons who lived within thirty miles of the accident). Assuming that these exclusions left a workable number of names, each would be questioned and his vehicle examined for signs of recent damage. At the same time, all garages and shops would be asked if, since Sunday, they had supplied a headlamp glass or unit or sold a touching-up spray can of the appropriate colour paint. Inevitably, his Escort would be listed and someone would ask to look at it, making it quite obvious that this was only for form's sake since no policeman would ever try to run away from an accident in which he'd been involved...

*   *   *

When Stone returned home, Andrew was out and June was upstairs, lying down. He sat on the edge of the bed. 'One of your thumping heads?'

'No.'

'Then what's the trouble?'

83

'You don't understand? How can you be so unfeeling?' Her voice trembled. 'Andy says you went on and on at him because you won't believe a word he tells you.'

'I wanted to see if he'd contradict himself.'

'Because you're so sure he's a liar?'

'Because I needed to find out if he was probably lying. His story didn't change in one single respect.'

'So?'

'Had he been lying, I should have expected at least one or two inconsistencies.'

She stared at him, brown eyes wide as if she were trying to reach into his mind to read it. 'Are you saying that at last you do believe him?'

'I questioned the staff at the four pubs nearest to where the accident happened and showed them Andy's photo—no one served him. I drove to the quarry and found an empty bottle of whisky and it had been handled by someone wearing gloves; that's sufficiently unusual to be significant.'

'Then all that proves he's telling the truth!'

'It proves nothing. Perhaps Andy managed to memorize his lies well enough to avoid inconsistencies; the bottle of whisky was dumped there the day before the accident and whoever handled it wore gloves because he has a skin complaint; and above all, what possible motive can there be for falsely implicating Andy in a hit-and-run?'

84

'There has to be one.'

'What is it?'

'I don't know,' she shouted wildly.

And nor did he. Accept that Andrew had not been caught up in the deadly world of drugs, then one had to uncover a recent event in which he had been involved which could have such disastrous consequences for someone that he had to be falsely implicated, either to sideline him or for revenge. The only recent and unusual event of any consequence was his accidental meeting with the would-be burglar outside Elsett Court. No such burglar would resort to so complicated a scheme merely to gain his revenge (and how would he have known who Andrew was?) Would Ogilvy (forget for the moment that as far as could be judged, he knew nothing about the incident) ever go to such lengths to punish the man who'd dishonoured his daughter? (Could 'dishonour' be realistically used?)

'There has to be a motive,' she said, even more insistently than before.

Since that seemed impossible, the evidence suggested Andrew was a liar. Yet looked at as a father, not a policeman, one remembered that humans often acted illogically and therefore their motives for those actions were equally illogical, and one could just about try to believe him ... 'June, the lad in the accident is in a critical condition so it's odds on that this is going to become a major case. The DI has already asked Swansea for a list of possible cars and this means one of the boys will want to check over ours.'

'Why?'

'To see if it's suffered a broken headlamp and a scratch on one of the panels.'

'Then repair the light.'

'It's not that easy. Inquiries will be made at all local garages and accessory stores to find out if anyone on the list has had a lamp unit repaired or renewed or has bought the paint to touch up.'

'Then you're saying ... You're saying that if nothing's done, they're going to believe it was our car in the accident?'

'I'm afraid that's right.'

'Oh my God!' She began to cry.

He moved until he could hug her to himself. The protective shield was cracking. He dare not let it shatter.

CHAPTER NINE

There was a sharp change of weather on Wednesday; the east wind had a bite to it and the thickening, black-bellied clouds suggested rain might arrive well before it was forecast.

As soon as he'd finished breakfast, Stone hurried upstairs. Andrew was asleep and it took several sharp shakes on the shoulder to awaken him. 'What's up?' he asked thickly.

'Listen very hard to what I'm going to say.'

'Not another bloody lecture...'

'I'm not here to lecture, but to give you your battle orders. Get up now and take the first train to London. There, buy a headlamp unit and a spray can of paint for our car.'

'Why bother to go all that way when I can get 'em at Lampley's?'

'Because we have to cover our tracks. A list is being drawn up of cars which fit the description the police have and ours is going to appear on it. Every car will be examined for signs of damage which tie it in with the hit-and-run. We have to eliminate those signs, remembering that the police will question all local garages and accessory stores to find out if anyone's bought a headlamp unit and the right colour paint. Do you understand now?'

'Yes, but...'

'No time for buts. We'll only have the one chance to cover up, they'll have as many chances as they want to uncover. One of the advantages of being a cop is that I know exactly how the case will move.' He tried to speak lightly, but failed because he could not hide his betrayal from himself. 'When you get back here, make certain the car's facing the house when you mend the light and the road when you paint out the scratch because that'll give you the cover of the hedge. Whenever you're about to screw in, dip the tip of the screwdriver in a mixture of egg yolk and vinegar—that helps to age the marks. Once the new unit is in place, cover the chrome with very fine earth, wash that off, and repeat several times. Spread oily gunge over all electrical connections you've handled.

'Don't just touch up the scratch on the rear door; rub down and then touch up half a dozen other places, including the tailgate, where rusting could well have occurred. When the paint's thoroughly dry, rub castor sugar over it until you've aged it as far as you can.

'Finally, collect up the tools and any rags you've used and take them out to the Bridgeworth dump ... Have you got all that?'

Andrew nodded.

*   *   *

Steven Hutton died at two-fifteen on Thursday afternoon.

Kemp was a compassionate man, yet his first reaction when given the news was one of annoyance. This was now a case to which, despite all the existing pressures of work, further resources must be allocated since it would receive considerably more publicity in the local press and one of the left-wing councillors had made it his task to explore what he was pleased to call police inefficiencies.

He mentally reviewed the few known facts. At the time of the collision, there had been no oncoming vehicles so that the overtaking car had had most of the road free—that he had hit the motorbike suggested the driver had been very drunk indeed. It seemed reasonable to suppose that a man (the DI was a closet sexist; he did not accept that women became drunk) in that condition could only have been driving for a short while, otherwise he would have had an accident earlier. While he might have been drinking in a private house, equally he might have been drinking in a pub.

The DI used the internal phone to order a DC to visit all the pubs in the area of Westbreak Road and to ask the staff if any of them had served a man very much the worse for wear on Saturday night, some time prior to eleven o'clock.

* * *

On Friday morning, Detective-Constable Masefield entered Stone's room with a rush. 'This has just been faxed through to us.' He put four sheets of paper down on the desk, turned and headed for the door.

'Hang on.'

'No can do.'

When Masefield was around, Stone thought, the bull in the china shop always came to mind. It was often something of a surprise to rediscover that beneath the carefree, bumptious manner was a shrewd mind.

The pages contained a list of seventy-two names and addresses. A note gave the categories of vehicles which had been eliminated—goods, earth-moving, etc.

He went through to the DI's office, found it empty, and was about to leave when the DI came along the corridor.

'Yes?' said Kemp, as he walked past Stone to enter the room. His manner was abrupt, but not discourteous; it spoke of a desire to make full use of every minute, not to impress his seniority.

'We've the list from DVLC, sir.'

The DI sat, held out his hand.

'I've done no more than skim through, but we should be able, at least initially, to eliminate quite a few on the score of colour.'

'Let's hope you're right or the job'll tie up half the force . . . Start checking, but remember colours look different at night.' He pushed the pages back across the desk.

Stone picked them up. 'By the way, I noticed my car's down here. I thought the number looked familiar!'

The DI showed his surprise. 'You didn't realize before now that it came within the given registration letters?'

'I can't say I did. It's a case of I knew the car wasn't involved, so I just never connected. One doesn't in this kind of situation . . . How many hands do I put on checking?'

'As many as are free.'

'That's none.'

'Get it done as soon as possible.' The DI's voice had sharpened; he did not appreciate pointless conversation.

*   *   *

CID aide Alfred Brenner hadn't yet learned to develop the thick hide that was the hallmark of a good detective and his embarrassment was obvious. 'I'm sorry, Sarge, but ... Well, it's like this, I've been given a list of cars I'm to examine ...'

Stone smiled. 'I gave it to you,'

'Yeah, of course! Only seeing it's your car, it doesn't seem ...' He tailed off into an uncomfortable silence.

'Come on inside and have a beer.'

'I don't think so, thanks all the same. I'm meant to check as many as possible on the list and it's all taking time ...'

'The wife's out in the car doing some late shopping, but she'll be back in maybe a quarter of an hour. That leaves you with time for a drink because it'll be quicker in the long run to hang on instead of going away and returning later. I'd suggest bringing the car to the station tomorrow morning, only Andy's booked it. When you've a son old enough to drive, you discover your car's not your own.' It would be far better to have the Escort examined at home than at the station—policemen made a sharp distinction between work and home and always tried to leave their suspicions at work. June would have said that that did not always happen.

They went into the sitting-room and Stone poured out two lagers. Knowing Brenner was a keen fisherman, he asked about the fishing on the coast that summer and was regaled with the usual hard luck story of the thirty-pound cod that almost, but not quite, came to hook.

Stone heard the sound of a car door. 'That's the wife.' He stood, left the room and met June as she stepped into the hall, a plastic carrier bag in her left hand. 'Hullo, love. Alfie's here to have a look at the car and make certain it wasn't any of us who knocked the poor devil off his motorbike.'

Her expression became panicky.

'Let me carry that for you.' He took the carrier bag and guided her into the kitchen. 'Stay in here.' He saw she was trembling. 'No cause for worry. Alfie's so embarrassed, he wouldn't notice if half the car were bashed in.'

He left, thankful he had been able to intercept her in time. Brenner might be inexperienced, but that probably wouldn't have stopped his correctly identifying her fear.

Back in the sitting-room, he said: 'How about the other half?'

'Not if that was your car come back; thanks all the same. I'll have a quick eyeball and then push on.'

'A glutton for work!'

Brenner grinned.

They went outside. The Escort, slightly damp from a brief shower, was parked facing the house. Brenner first checked the headlamps, paying close attention to the surrounds, then the bodywork. 'Looks like you've been doing a bit of patching, Sarge?'

'Is it that obvious? I hoped I'd done a better job. Not long back, I found some rust on the tailgate and that started me checking and before I'd finished I'd found half a dozen places that needed attention. You'd have thought that by now they'd have learned to build a car that didn't rust before it's five years old.'

'They say it's the salt what gets put down on the roads during snow times ... When d'you reckon you did that work?'

Stone shrugged his shoulders. 'I first meant to do it back in the Spring, but what with one thing and another, I suppose it can't have been much more than a month since.'

'So it was before Sunday.' It was a comment, not a question. 'That's fine, then. Sorry to have bothered you, Sarge, and thanks for the drink.'

Brenner left in the CID Montego. Stone went through to the kitchen. June, standing by the table, said shrilly: 'What happened?'

'He came, he saw, he concurred.'

'How can you joke about it?'

'Didn't you know that a pun a day keeps the

truth at bay?'

* * *

Wearing stared at the mirror behind the bar and not for the first time wondered why he had inherited his father's gloomy expression and not his mother's laughing one.

'Minnie says you wants a word. Make it snappy, will you? Sunday morning's always a rush.' The landlord of the Seven Sisters was large, round, and not in the least worried by his beer stomach; he was noted for an apparently endless fund of blue jokes and even bluer limericks.

'I'm interested in who was here last Saturday evening?'

'The world and his wife, thank God! With the brewers putting up the rent into high orbit, if we're not solid with customers, I'm shaking hands with bankruptcy.'

'You look as if you've reserves.'

The landlord patted his stomach.

'Can you remember anyone that night who was really tight—probably some little time before eleven?'

'Bloody hell! Haven't you blokes anything to do but stop a man earning an honest living by asking him the same questions over and over again?'

'How d'you mean?'

'Your detective-sergeant was in here

94

Tuesday afternoon with the same problem and asking if any of us could recognize the photo he showed. I told him then, as I'm telling you now, if anyone gets half way plastered, I chuck him out.'

'So there was no one in here who was noticeably drunk?'

'That's what I'm saying. Is that all? . . . Then I'll get back to work. If you'd fancy a pint, tell Tilly.' He turned and walked up the bar, had a quick word with the younger of the barmaids, patted her fondly on the bottom, moved on.

Tilly came down to where Wearing stood. She was not as young as she would have liked to be thought; she was far too old for her neckline. 'Barney says to give you a pint of the best if you'd like.'

'I'll not say no.'

'Never met a man who could.'

*　　　*　　　*

Kemp returned from the monthly conference at county HQ in a bad temper, which was not unusual. The assistant chief constable (east) never used one word where three could spread out and the detective chief superintendent suffered from indigestion.

He sat, looked at the pile of paperwork which had accumulated since that morning, and rang his wife to say he'd be home late. Her comment, 'Why not save on the phone bills and just ring on the odd occasion you do decide to come home at a reasonable hour,' did nothing to improve his temper.

He used the internal phone to speak to Stone, but there was no answer. He called the CID general room. 'Where's the DS?'

Wearing answered. 'I think he had to go out to Rennington Green, sir.'

'I want to see him the moment he gets back.'

'I'll leave a message.'

'Have you been round all the pubs?'

'A couple more to go, sir, and as they won't be opening until later on, I'm waiting for when they do.'

'Any result so far?'

'There's no one remembers a drunk. One or two customers were cheerful, but that's all. Like the landlord of the Seven Sisters said to the Sarge and me, if anyone looks like getting real tight, out he goes for fear of losing the licence.'

'You'd think to listen to 'em that they all wore bloody haloes.' He replaced the receiver. It had been a very long longshot. He picked up a ballpoint pen, read and signed the first of the forms in front of him, realized there was something he wanted to raise with Wearing. He dialled the general room again.

'It's Brenner, sir.' One could almost hear him coming to seated attention.

'Put Wearing on.'

'I'm afraid he's just left the room.'

'The story of my life!' He slammed down the receiver.

* * *

Kemp was three-quarters of the way through the paperwork when there was a knock on the door. Wearing entered. 'I've been to the last of the pubs, sir, but there's nothing.'

'So do we call it a dead end or do we enlarge the area?'

Recognizing that this was a rhetorical question, Wearing did not try to answer it.

Kemp mulled the problem over in his mind. A successful detective had to learn not to pursue a possible lead if that had started to look very tired, just out of stubbornness. If, contrary to what seemed probable, the driver of the hit-and-run car had been able to drive a distance without coming to grief, then he could have been drinking on the outskirts of town or in the countryside; it would take far too many man-hours to check all possible pubs. 'All right,' he said dismissively.

'Sir?'

'What?'

'Brenner told me you wanted a word.'

It took him a couple of seconds to remember. 'Over the phone earlier on you said the DS was with you when you talked to the landlord of the Seven Sisters. Why the devil did it take two of you to do the job?'

'It didn't, sir. The Sarge was there on Tuesday afternoon.'

'Asking the same questions?'

'That, and showing 'em a photo of someone.'

'Did the landlord know who the photograph was of?'

'No, sir.'

'Thanks.'

Kemp ran a crooked forefinger along his right eyebrow, a frequent mannerism of his. Stone had obviously moved very quickly and on his own initiative, which was not unusual. But what was slightly surprising was the fact that he had not informed Wearing there was no need to bother with the Seven Sisters since that had already been covered. And a photograph meant he had a definite man in mind, yet he'd made no mention of a suspect. Was the driver a criminal who'd been fingered by an informer? A detective tried never to pass on news obtained from a fingering until reasonably certain it was good...

Kemp had almost finished his work and was therefore in sight of returning home when, to his irritation, he found that an unidentified memory was upsetting his concentration. Something had been mentioned which contradicted something else ... Goddamn all somethings!

*   *   *

'Wouldn't it be an idea to go to bed?' Marie asked.

Kemp opened his eyes and stared at his wife, who was knitting a patterned sweater for their younger daughter. He looked away and at the television. 'I thought it was supposed to be the travel film?'

'That finished five minutes ago.'

'Blast! I wanted to watch it.'

'I tried to wake you when it started, but all you could do was to tell me to B off.'

He grinned. 'I must have been dreaming I was at the office.' Many of his juniors would have been surprised to learn that at home he relaxed and was often light-hearted.

'I suppose it's too much to ask you at least to forget work when you dream?'

He yawned. 'I need a break. How about a cruise in the Caribbean?'

'If I thought you meant it, I'd make you book tomorrow.' She reached the end of the row, slid the knitting down to the end of one needle, pushed both into the ball of wool. She used the remote control to switch off the television. 'Come on, make the move.' She stood, put the knitting into a large cane basket, checked that nothing in the room needed tidying before they went upstairs, crossed to the door, looked back. 'You really are hopeless!' she said in tones of exasperation. 'You're so tired you slept right through that programme, yet when it's time for bed, you won't move.'

'It's just...'

'Let me guess. Something to do with work?'

He had the grace to look shamefaced. 'Something's been nibbling at my mind and I can't identify what it is.'

'The best way of remembering something is deliberately to forget it.'

'I always knew that your mother was more Irish than English.'

*   *   *

He was stuck in a traffic jam at the bottom of Bank Street and mentally cursing the local council who had refused to follow the police's suggestion for better vehicle circulation, when he remembered what it was he had been trying to identify the previous evening.

He finally reached divisional HQ. In his office, he used the internal phone to ask for the movements books for all CID cars. He found the reference he sought in the Renault's log which, along with the others, he had OK'd on the Saturday. On Tuesday, the twentieth, Stone had signed on at 1315 hours and off at 1703, listing investigations into the Trebarth case. But that was a burglary and assault which had taken place four miles north of the town and according to Wearing, Stone had been making inquiries at the Seven Sisters in south-east Peteringham. So it seemed the entry had to be wrong, either by commission or omission. Odd. Yet if a detective cultivated a really valuable informer, he could become paranoid about concealing his identity ... Kemp decided not to pursue the matter.

CHAPTER TEN

A notable politician had written, 'Time is the great physician.' (He neglected to add, how else would any politician ever be re-elected?) By Saturday, June no longer had shadows in her eyes and a telephone call or a knock on the door did not start her heart thumping.

She climbed out of bed, crossed to the window and drew the curtains. 'I've a wonderful idea.'

'With the sun on the other side of your nightdress, I've a pretty good one myself,' Stone said.

'You know perfectly well that you have to be out of the house in twenty minutes so if we don't get up right away, you'll miss breakfast.'

'I'll forgo eggs if I can enjoy some bacon.'

'Do try and lift your mind onto a different track.'

'Then move away from the window.'

She moved. 'You did say it was your afternoon off?'

'Provided there isn't a sudden flood of work.

Like scores of frustrated husbands committing suicide.' He climbed out of bed.

'Let's all three of us have a late picnic lunch down on the beach.'

He began to dress. 'You don't think that Andy's at an age when the attractions of bucket and spade have been overtaken by other, potentially more exciting ones?'

'That one-track mind again! Of course he'd like to be with us. He's suffering from a bruised ego and that's why a picnic would be such a good idea. It'll help him regain his equilibrium.'

He thought she was wrong on every count, but did not argue any further for fear of upsetting her rediscovered pleasure in life.

*　　*　　*

Kemp stared through the window at the vicarage. His mind drifted and conjured up the deck of a cruise liner, the tang of salt air, and a smudge on the horizon that was an exotically tropical island ... Imagination retreated and his sense of the practical returned. By the time he retired, even if he could afford such a trip, he'd far prefer to remain at home, feet up, telly on ...

Masefield knocked and entered. 'I've got the reports.' He waved the sheaf of papers in his right hand.

'Is one allowed to know what they're about?'

Kemp asked sarcastically.

'The inquiries concerning the hit-and-run, sir,' replied Masefield with undiminished gusto.

'Well?'

'No car with a bust headlamp or scratch, no sale of a headlamp unit, and no recorded sale of touch-up paint.'

Masefield put the papers down on the desk, left. Kemp returned to his chair, read through them. It quickly became clear that the inquiries had been carried out by two detectives since roughly half were far more detailed than was necessary. It needed little prescience on his part to decide that the more detailed ones had been compiled by Brenner...

He clipped the reports together. It was, he thought with sharp annoyance, going to become an LP case. Unsolved through lack of proof. But the local media, egged on by that bastard left-wing councillor, would delight in presenting the failure as due to incompetence. At work, a policeman was meant to be politically neutral, but it was difficult to live up to that ideal when one knew that the force was being wrongly criticized in order to break down its morale; destroy the police and law and order must go; without either, the extremists had it made ... His mind flicked away and after a moment's thought, he searched through the reports for the one concerning Stone's car. He read it through far more carefully than before. The Escort's headlights had been undamaged and there was no indication of recent work on either. The paintwork had been touched-up at seven points—three on the near-side, one on the boot, one on the tailgate, two on the off-side. When questioned, Detective-Sergeant Stone had stated that the work had been necessary because of rusting; it had been carried out approximately a month ago. Appearances were consistent with the time stated. The stilted phraseology and the unnecessary details named this as one of Brenner's reports.

Cars rusted, as every owner knew to his cost, and so if sensible he took quick remedial action to counter it. On the face of things, there was nothing significant in Stone's actions. But one of the best ways of hiding a single point of damage was to draw attention to it while at the same time dismissing the possibility that it was relevant...

When he'd discovered that Stone had incorrectly written up the log of the Renault, he'd instinctively provided a reasonable explanation—instinctively, because the Detective-Sergeant was a trusted member of the team. But the incorrect entry had concealed the fact that Stone had been making inquiries into the hit-and-run and asking for identification of a photograph when there was presumably no known suspect...

Kemp tried to convince himself he was

building with straw. Time and again Stone had proved himself to be a loyal member of the team ... But what if he were faced by a second loyalty, diametrically opposed to the first? Which would he then honour?

* * *

No one liked it, all would have been happy to see it discontinued, but tradition dictated that every year F Division held a social at which families were not only invited, but expected to attend. It was the only Saturday afternoon when there were volunteers for extra duty.

Kemp opened the album of photographs—paid for by the divisional social fund—which had been taken the previous summer and turned the pages until he found a photograph of the Stone family. Stone held a glass in his hand, June was trying to smile but looking uneasy, even a shade bewildered, and their son—what was his name?—was plainly bored.

Kemp eased the photograph out of its mounting. One didn't need much imagination to understand how tragically a person like June Stone would be affected by a threat to her family.

* * *

Kemp rang home to say that he was very sorry, but something had suddenly turned up and he was going to be delayed. Marie replied that he was not going to be delayed because they had a dinner date which he had promised faithfully to keep and then she slammed down the receiver. He sighed. But he couldn't detail one of the DCs to make the inquiries because he was not yet certain that his suspicions had any real base ... He wondered if the homemade chocolate shop in Wedmore Street would still be open? A check on the time showed it would not. Homecoming was going to be very difficult.

He left HQ and drove through the maze of streets in south-east Peteringham to the Seven Sisters. The saloon bar had not, he was pleased to discover, been tarted up to resemble an English interior decorator's idea of a Tyrolean wine garden. The barmaid poured him out a gin and tonic and as she handed him the glass, he said he'd like a word with the landlord. She left, surprised that he had not tried to look down the front of her dress.

The landlord came along the bar. 'So what can I do for you?'

'CID.'

The landlord's expression soured. 'Seems like you blokes haven't anything to do but come in here for freebies.'

'I paid for this gin.'

'You'll be needing a refill.'

'If I do, I'll be paying for that as well.'

'Makes a change.'

'Just under a fortnight ago, one of my chaps came in here and asked if you could identify a photograph.'

The landlord, remembering that the police could become very subtle when they explained to the magistrates why they believed the renewal of a liquor licence would be a bad thing, recalled his normal, mine-host bonhomie. 'That's right.'

'Would you recognize him again?'

'I've a memory for faces.'

'Then have a butcher's at this and tell me if it was he.' Kemp brought out the photograph, taken from the album, and used an old envelope to blot out June and Andrew.

'That's him.'

Kemp upended the photograph so that it was no longer visible to the landlord, moved the envelope until Andrew was exposed, but June remained hidden. 'Is this the same person who was in the photo he showed you?'

'That's right.' The landlord scratched the third of his chins. 'This other bloke had stuck paper over part of his photo. So what's so secret?'

'A full frontal.'

When Kemp returned to his car, he sat behind the wheel but did not immediately switch on the engine. He swore crudely, something he rarely did. If a detective went crooked, this reflected badly on his superior even when it was in no way the latter's fault, but it was not this which caused him to swear—it was that Stone, by choosing to avoid Scylla, must be sucked down by Charybdis.

CHAPTER ELEVEN

The church bells were ringing, to remind people it was Sunday when Stone entered Kemp's room and, at a sign, sat in front of the desk.

'Twelve days ago, you used the CID Renault and wrote in the log that you were conducting inquiries into the Trebarth case. Was that correct?' It was an indirect approach because Kemp was hoping that Stone would confess voluntarily which must count in his favour.

Stone tried to conceal his sudden uneasiness. 'Yes, sir.'

'Were those the only inquiries you carried out that afternoon?'

Stone found himself in the classic position of a suspect who couldn't judge how much of the truth his questioner knew, rather than suspected, but who had to accept that the other must have some knowledge to have posed the question. 'As a matter of fact, no, they weren't.'

'What other case or cases were you investigating?'

'The hit-and-run in Westbreak Road.'

'What line were you pursuing?'

'I'd had a buzz and wanted to check it out.'

'What was that?'

'It came through a grass.'

'Which doesn't answer my question.'

'It was a possible identification.'

'Who was the man identified?'

'It turned out to be a wrong finger, so I'd rather not answer in order to keep my source clean.'

'Why wasn't this inquiry noted in the log?'

'Like I've just said, it was a bummer so since the trip hardly took me out of my way, it didn't seem worth recording.'

'The break-in was four miles north of town. The Seven Sisters is in south-east Peteringham.'

Stone was shocked by the naming of the public house. 'I was really thinking in terms of time, not distance.'

'Then presumably the roads were free of traffic, since normally that diversion would take a long time?'

'They were pretty empty, yes.'

'What did you do at the pub?'

'Asked a few questions.'

'That was all?'

'I also showed the staff a photo. They failed to identify it.'

'A photo of whom?'

'The man who was fingered.'

'You're quite certain of that?'

'Yes, sir.'

'Then it was your son who was named?'

There was a long silence which allowed them to become aware of the sounds of the outside world. The bells, Stone noted with that strange irrelevance which could accompany a moment of great tension, were still sounding. 'Are you suggesting something?' he asked thickly.

'I am suggesting that it was your car which was involved in the accident and that it was your son, under the influence, who was driving it. I'm further suggesting that from the moment you discovered the truth, you've done everything possible to conceal it.'

'Are you making a formal accusation?'

'Goddamnit, man, can't you see that I'm doing everything I can to give you the chance to confess of your own accord in order that you gain the benefit of that?'

'Some benefit, when I'd be accusing my own son!'

Kemp stood, pushed back his chair, walked round the desk to the window and stared out. 'I've always done my best to live my working life according to the standards demanded. But that doesn't mean I can't understand that there can be a time when a man is faced either with betraying those standards or someone he loves. God knows how he decides which. But knowing a man has been faced with an impossible choice, does not and cannot absolve me from carrying out my duty if his decision breaks the law.'

'An easy let-out for the conscience.'

He swung round. 'You're not a fool, so don't talk like one.' He returned to his seat. 'Did you show the staff at the Seven Sisters a photograph of your son?'

'I showed the landlord a photo that was not of my son.'

'He has identified your son as the subject.'

'Then he's made a mistake. Perhaps because he was misled into making it.'

'Insults don't help.'

'If it's an insult merely to suggest that you may have inadvertently fed him the wrong signals, how does one rate your deliberate and totally unjust accusation?'

Kemp spoke with bitter resignation. 'Very well. You've made it clear how you want to play things. I should like your permission to have your car examined to discover whether it bears signs of having been involved in an accident.'

'And if I refuse?'

'You surely don't need to ask?'

An order would be obtained and the granting of it would ensure far more publicity than would be generated by his voluntarily agreeing. Such publicity would harm his family, himself, and his career, even if nothing could be proved. 'All right.'

'Put your permission in writing.'

'In case I turn round and call you a liar?'

Kemp went to speak, checked the words. Then he said, trying not to sound angry: 'Sign it and add date, time, and place.'

Stone wondered how many times he had said that to possible suspects.

*　　　*　　　*

Throughout his drive home, Stone had racked his brains to discover some way of breaking the news to June without frightening her; by the time he parked in front of the house, he'd come to the obvious conclusion—there wasn't one. He entered and went through to the kitchen, determined to tell her immediately because what couldn't be avoided was better met head on. Ironically, he found her to be in a bubbling humour.

'Hullo, love.' She had to speak loudly because she was using the Kenwood mixer. 'I'm making that chocolate pudding with ground almonds you liked so much at the Tibbits'. And I've even bought a carton of cream to have with it, despite that article in the paper about the terrible dangers of cholesterol in the over-forties. So you can give me an extra special kiss.'

He did so.

'Mary rang earlier—guess what she told me?'

He simply did not have the heart—or was it courage?—to destroy her cheerfulness. 'With

112

her, it's impossible to guess what she'll say next.'

'Derek and Patsy are going out together.'

'In a pig's ear! Derek forswore the female sex even before he reached puberty.'

'Don't be so beastly. It's positively Neanderthal to go on thinking a man's a queer just because he uses scent.' She switched off the mixer. 'Instead of standing there, talking like you were a blinkered ninety-three-year-old, remember it's Sunday evening. I'll have a gin and tonic, please, and don't mind letting your hand shake when you pour the gin. I feel like getting slightly woofy.'

He poured out the drinks in the pantry, returned to the kitchen and handed her a glass.

'I'm sure I'm an incipient alcoholic because I enjoy a drink so much.'

'I've never seen anyone less likely ever to become a lush.'

'Then I'll drown my fears ... I'll put the pudding on to steam and then we can go through to the other room.' She used a plastic spatula to transfer the mixture into a bowl, fitted a lid on that and put it into a large saucepan in which the water was gently boiling. 'By the way, Andy's not in for supper.'

'Does that mean that Joanna's back?'

'I'm pretty certain not. No, he's with Henry, doing something with computers. Kate, Henry's sister, is such a nice girl; a good cook and coming from a home where every penny

113

has to count, she'll know how to run things properly.'

'Have you booked the church?'

'That's right, laugh at me! Sometimes I wonder why I married you.'

It was a question she might ask herself again and again if both he and Andrew were found guilty...

'Why are you looking like that? For heaven's sake, you know I was only joshing you.' She came forward and kissed him. 'I married you because you are the most wonderful man in the world. Only I don't like to tell you too often in case you become swollen headed.'

*   *   *

Time and again, he'd had to break the news that a husband/wife/son/daughter had had an accident and was either seriously ill or dead, yet however painful those experiences, they had not inured him to what he had to do now. He stood at the foot of the bed. 'There's something you need to know.'

She was already in bed, but instead of opening a book and reading, she lay on her back and stared at him with shining eyes. It was a signal. 'Tell me afterwards.'

He shook his head.

'Don't be such a killjoy. Or isn't it fun for you any more?' She spoke teasingly. All too often, her world was darkness, so when it was all light...

He sat on the edge of the bed. 'Something serious has happened. The accident's come alive again.'

She shivered and the light went out of her deep brown eyes. 'But ... but you said it wouldn't do that because there was no proof.'

'Somehow the guv'nor's found out I went to a pub and showed Andy's photo to the landlord.'

'How can that matter?'

'It means I was trying to discover if Andy had been drinking there on the night of the hit-and-run. I wouldn't have been doing that unless I'd reason to think he'd been driving our car and run down the motorcyclist. The guv'nor asked me to give permission for our car to be examined by Vehicles.'

'But you refused?'

'No.'

Her voice rose. 'For God's sake, why not?'

'He'd just have obtained an order compelling me to release it for examination.'

She swallowed heavily. 'They'll not be able to find out anything, will they? You made certain of that?'

'Yes.' But he couldn't stop himself remembering how often criminals were convicted on evidence they'd been so certain they had destroyed.

CHAPTER TWELVE

The report from Vehicles arrived on Wednesday. Kemp read it through. His suspicions were confirmed, but conclusive proof was not yet available; it was hoped that the forensic laboratory would provide that.

He cursed a world in which an honest man could be forced into making a dishonest decision. Then he rang county HQ and asked for an appointment with the detective chief superintendent.

*   *   *

Abbott was something of a misnomer. An abbot should be a thin, austere man, concerned with things spiritual not temporal, honouring principle not practice; Detective Chief Superintendent Abbott was fat, hedonistic, far more interested in his flesh than his soul, and a pragmatist to the tips of his roly-poly fingers. Being the man he was, he blamed a malign fate for his chronic indigestion, not his eating habits. 'I don't like it,' he said.

He didn't like anything which threatened to upset his peace, Kemp thought.

'Damnit, it's neither one thing nor the other.' He slapped the palm of his hand down on the report which lay on the desk.

'It confirms it was Stone's car which was involved in the hit-and-run and that someone tried to cover up the evidence of this.'

'Would you like to take the case to court solely on this report?'

'No, sir.'

'Then it proves nothing.'

'I did say "confirm", not prove.'

Abbott stared at Kemp with dislike.

'If, as they hope, they can go on specifically to match the paint found on the handlebars with the paint from Stone's car, it'll virtually become an open-and-shut case.'

'If ... Assuming the shattered headlamp was replaced by Stone, why haven't you traced where the replacement was bought?'

Kemp stifled a sigh. 'Extensive inquiries have been made locally, unfortunately without result.'

'Why only locally?'

'Because at the time that seemed logical. Now we know that it was Stone's car, we can be certain he'll not have purchased the unit locally. If authorized, I could put out a country-wide request for help in tracing the source, but obviously the odds are against success.'

Such a request would be very unpopular with all the other forces; Abbott did not answer the unasked question. 'So where do you go from here with regard to Stone?'

'I was hoping to have your advice as to that,'

117

replied Kemp.

It was a tricky situation. The rules were clear. A police officer suspected of a criminal offence had to be suspended on full pay while an investigation was carried out. But what the rules failed to define was the extent to which the suspicion had to be supported by hard evidence before suspension was invoked. The officer who ordered a suspension which turned out to be unwarranted earned not only a very large black mark on his record, but also the sharp dislike of his peers. The officer who did not order a suspension which later events proved earned not only a very large black mark on his record, but also the sharp dislike of his superiors.

Abbott had not reached high rank without developing a natural ability to side-step difficult decisions. 'Has Stone had all his annual leave this year?'

'Speaking from memory, no.'

'Then send him on leave.'

*　　　*　　　*

Stone left the DI's room and went along the corridor to his own. He sat behind the desk and stared at the far wall. A fortnight's leave, to be taken immediately. He didn't need to be smart to appreciate that leave was a euphemism for suspension or that there was not yet sufficient proof for suspension, but the odds all were that soon there would be. He felt like a man strapped in to a car with duff brakes, heading downhill towards the edge of a high cliff...

Goddamnit, truth wasn't necessarily strangled by a cliché. Where there was life, there was hope. He stood and went through to the general room, spoke to Masefield and Younger. 'Did either of you collect the report from Traffic on the fatal hit-and-run?' He saw no hint of embarrassment in their manner. Clearly, care had been taken by the author of the report to conceal the identity of the car's owner.

'It came through on fax, Sarge, and I passed it on to the guv'nor.' Younger was knocking middle age, disillusioned, and looking forward to retirement.

'So what's in it?'

If he was surprised that Stone had not seen the report, he did not show this. 'Boiled down, that's the car which was involved, but they can't yet prove it.'

'What is there left to do?'

'There's some complicated test the lab's got to carry out on the paint and it's going to be difficult because they recovered so little from the bike.'

'Did they give any kind of a time-scale?'

'No.'

He switched the conversation and discussed the poor performance of the divisional cricket team. Ten minutes later he returned to his room and spoke to Vehicles at county HQ. What about the paint? They referred him to the forensic laboratory which was now dealing with it. He phoned the laboratory and a woman, earnestly enthusiastic about her job, answered his question. The first difficulty was the pressure of work, which meant it would be some time before they could start the tests; the second was the very small crime sample, virtually pulverized, with which they'd been provided. However, there was reason to hope that with the new techniques ... She spoke about scanning microscopes, setting flakes of paint in blocks of epoxy resin glue to provide cross-sections, bombarding with beams of high energy electrons, and chemical analysis; she became almost ecstatic about the virtues of gas chromatography mass spectrometry...

Eventually, she had to pause. 'So as I understand things,' he said, 'it's going to be some time before you can give us a definite report?'

'Certainly not less than one week; much more realistically, probably between two and three weeks.'

After thanking her and ringing off, he fiddled with a pencil. Assume the worst—the policeman's motto, genuflect to Sod's Law— and he only had one week before the laboratory provided the proof that it was his Escort which had been involved in the hit-and-run...

Why had Andrew been framed? If he'd asked himself that once, he'd asked it ten-dozen times. And never been able to provide an answer that made good sense. He'd trawled through everything which had happened to Andrew in the recent past and the only incident that could by any imagination be significant was the confrontation with the would-be burglar outside Elsett Court. Superficially, it could seem that this incident might have a bearing on subsequent events. But after being so unexpectedly surprised, the burglar would have got the hell as far away as he could—and the last thing he'd have considered doing would have been to return in order to execute an elaborate frame-up of Andrew. And how could he have known Andrew would be a legitimate visitor at Elsett Court the next evening?

Frustrated, about to give up trying to pin down something that would stay beyond reach, Stone remembered the grizzled sergeant at the training college who'd unashamedly commandeered the wisdom of others. When, he'd said, brushing his Kitchener moustache, you've eliminated the impossible, what remains, however improbable, must be the truth. Then however improbable it might seem, the two events were connected. Andrew had caught no more than a glimpse of the burglar, but the latter could not be certain how clearly he had been seen—perhaps identification was the clue to motive. Yet if so critical, why had Andrew not been murdered then and there? Because the investigation following murder must prove too dangerous? . . . Look at events from the would-be burglar's viewpoint. It was a mirror image. He would have assumed Andrew was a would-be burglar, if mark one amateur, and that once he recovered consciousness he'd put as great a distance as possible between himself and Elsett Court. Only afterwards had he learned that Andrew had been a departing Romeo, not an arriving burglar. Such information could only have come from Ogilvy or Joanna—the servants were away. But even knowing that, why should Andrew prove so great a threat when it was obviously in his interests to keep the whole incident quiet? Because Andrew's father was a detective and when he heard what had happened to his son, his interest would be immediate even if, because of the circumstances, he did not initially initiate an investigation? So make certain that that interest never became focused by framing Andrew, leaving him unable to worry about anything else, least of all what was the truth behind the events of the night . . .

Suppositions based on a premise that was at best doubtful, at worst the product of desperation? . . . But then Stone remembered that Andrew had had a date with Joanna the following night, but when he'd driven to Elsett

122

Court to pick her up it had been to find that she'd stood him up. Stone might be wrong—June would say he was—but he judged that while Joanna would be indifferent to most conventions, normally she would never betray herself which meant that had she decided not to go to the party with Andrew, she would have told him so, face to face. Had she been 'persuaded' to leave in the morning because that evening she might inadvertently have told Andrew something potentially very dangerous? Such as the fact that very soon after he'd crept out of the house, they had had a totally unexpected visitor? ... If identification of this visitor had been a matter of such concern that an innocent motorcyclist would be mown down in order to conceal it, he surely had to be criminally important? So had there been any serious criminal incident on that Saturday which might point to his identity?

Stone left and went through to the general room; only Masefield was present. 'Where are last month's crime reports?'

'As far as I know, they're both on Frank's desk.'

Masefield's tone of voice and the fact that, having answered the question, he returned to his work rather than engaging in boisterous conversation, by choice about women, suggested that rumours about Stone's involvement in the hit-and-run were finally circulating. Grim-faced, Stone made his way to

Wearing's desk. On it were two loose-leaf folders, one very much thinner than the other; the first contained a summary of all county crimes, the second a summary of all serious crimes in the rest of the country, for July. He opened the country-wide folder at Saturday the seventeenth and began to skim through the reports. The fourth was given the coding G, which meant priority and that it had in addition been circulated to all airports and ports. Roger Illmore, serving eighteen months for receiving, had escaped from Torring Farm open prison, using a gun smuggled in to him. There were the usual photographs, in full face and in profile.

Stone had, of course, seen the report when it had first come through, but with the regrettable, if inevitable, indifference to other force's problems, had done no more than memorize Illmore's face. If he'd come face to face with him, he'd have identified and arrested him; but had he been asked to name the date of the escape, the prison involved, or the offence for which Illmore had been imprisoned, he wouldn't have been able to answer immediately...

He wondered why the case had been given a G coding? This indicated a very serious crime and that there was every reason for thinking the person named would be trying to flee the country. Yet a man convicted of receiving was normally a long way short of the big league...

124

He unclipped the three holding rings and extracted the report, went down to the general office to make a copy of it. Back in his room, he telephoned Essex county HQ, and spoke to the liaison officer and asked for a fax giving all available information on Illmore. 'By the way,' he added, 'if you can find out why a G notice was slapped on, I'd be grateful.'

Twenty minutes later, a cadet brought him the fax. Roger Illmore, 30 years old, born in Liverpool. No fixed address. Convicted of receiving and sentenced to eighteen months. No previous record. After psychological and general assessments, transferred to Torring Farm. Regarded as a model prisoner until the day of his escape. That Saturday, he'd had two visitors, a woman who'd claimed to be his sister and her child; it was presumed the gun had been smuggled to him with the help of the child. A Jaguar, later identified as having been stolen in Chelmsford, had picked him up outside the prison; that had been found abandoned two miles away. At 02.35, Sunday, a crashed BMW three miles south of Brentwood had been reported. This was subsequently found to have been stolen the previous afternoon in Hampstead. Traces of blood indicated at least one occupant had been injured in the crash. A tyre impression near the Jaguar virtually identified the BMW as the change-over car. There had been no subsequent sighting of Illmore. Inquiries in the area in which the BMW had crashed showed that a five-year-old, gold-coloured Ford Fiesta had been stolen that night; no provable connection between the Ford and Illmore had been established. It was not known why a G order had been made.

Stone brought a map of the south of England out of his desk. If one were driving from Carlington to Elsett Court, one would probably make for Dartford in order to cross the river and therefore Brentwood lay en route...

Yet what possible connection could there be between Ogilvy, a man of wealth and status, with a convicted, small-time criminal?

CHAPTER THIRTEEN

June, no longer the laughing, bubbling woman of the previous evening, was out shopping. Stone was in the dining-room, sitting at the table and making notes, when Andrew entered. 'Dad, what's happened? Mum's looking like her horoscope says she died last night. And you're not at work.'

He put down the pencil. 'I'm afraid that things have turned sour.'

'Oh!' Andrew fidgeted with the back of one of the chairs. 'What's that mean exactly?'

'Despite our best efforts with the car, there's

enough evidence almost, but not yet quite, to identify it as the one involved in the hit-and-run. Further tests at the forensic lab are likely to make it certain.'

'Then ... then what?'

'We'd be charged, for different offences.'

'But we couldn't be sent to jail?'

'In my case, a policeman who turns black is almost always jailed, *pour encourager les autres*. In your case, it would be a toss-up. Normally, first offenders aren't jailed, but causing death by reckless driving is a very serious offence, manslaughter even more so.'

'Oh Christ!' He swallowed heavily. 'But, Dad, I wasn't driving.'

'Innocence isn't always a solid defence.'

'They can't jail me for something I didn't do.'

'I'm afraid history is littered with innocent people who've been dealt injustice. You'll find it much easier to face the future if you accept the fact.' Clearly, Andrew was shocked by that. 'There's something you must come to terms with if you're to survive. The cavalry doesn't always come galloping along just in time to save one from the Indians. So our only hope is to start fighting to prove you're not guilty, rather than waiting for your innocence to save you.'

'But you've always said it's virtually impossible to prove a negative.'

'A change of words is easy. We have to fight

to prove you're innocent.'

'How, when you've tried to find a way and can't?'

'Miracles can still happen. But before we start to work out how to summon up our particular miracle, we need a drink to bolster our optimism. What will you have?'

'A whisky,' Andrew muttered.

Stone went through to the pantry where he poured out two whiskies, then returned to the dining-room. After handing Andrew one glass, he went round the table and picked up the copy of the crime report. 'Have a look at this man and tell me if he rings any bells.'

Andrew studied the rather grainy photographs. 'There could be something vaguely familiar about him.'

'No stronger than that?'

'Not really. Who is he?'

'Roger Illmore. He broke out of jail last month. It's possible he was the man you came face to face with outside Joanna's place.'

'The guy who knocked me out?' Andrew stared far more intently at the photograph. 'You know, I reckon that *is* him! That's why he seemed familiar, only I couldn't place him.'

It was far from being a good identification. Witnesses were forever suddenly becoming certain after learning there might well be cause for such certainty. But Stone said, 'Good,' in an encouraging tone as if something important had been established.

Andrew pulled out a chair and sat. He drank. 'Is there anything more?'

'Questions by the score. Did you tell me that when you went to pick up Joanna to go to the party and discovered she wasn't at home, Ogilvy was unusually friendly?'

Andrew was perplexed by the question, since it seemed irrelevant, but he answered readily enough. 'I expected him to say goodbye, good riddance. I mean, he's never put his arm around my shoulder and called me buddy-boy. But he asked me in, gave me a drink, and chatted away like he was glad to see me. I had quite a job to get away.'

'How long were you in the house?'

'I suppose it was nearly half an hour.'

Every detective was warned against composing a theory and then shuffling the facts to fit it but, Stone thought, nothing was being shuffled when he noted that half an hour was probably long enough to have ensured that Andrew could be followed and intercepted. 'Did he tell you where Joanna was?'

'Only that she and Betty had gone north to the Highlands, maybe stopping off at Betty's place on the way.'

'Do you know Betty?'

'Never met her and from the way Joanna talks, that's no loss. She sounds really weird— full of soul and all that sort of thing. Won't go anywhere or do anything without consulting her horoscope.'

'Don't let your mother hear you treat horoscopes in that tone of voice ... So you've no idea what Betty's surname is or where her parents live?'

'None at all. Is it important?'

'I'd like to get hold of Joanna and have a word with her.'

'Why?'

'To hear what, if anything, happened after you left the house that Saturday night ... Suppose you go back to Elsett Court and tell Ogilvy you very much want to get in touch with Joanna, can he please help? If he says he can't, ask him for the address of Betty's parents since they might know how to contact their daughter. It's possible he'll find a way of refusing, so listen to everything he says with both ears very wide open. A man can give a lot away without ever realizing that.'

'When d'you want me to go there?'

'Presumably he's at work during the day, so it'll have to be in the evening. Some time around eight when with any luck he'll have eaten and mellowed after a couple of glasses of port.'

'It would take a couple of bottles really to mellow him, Dad.'

It was good to hear Andrew once more speaking lightly.

*   *   *

Stone met June in the hall and carried the basket of shopping through to the kitchen. 'There's been a change of plan, love,' he said, as he put the basket on the table.

She said nothing. She was so frightened that the world was crushing her.

'I'm driving up to Carlington to see if I can have a chat with one or two blokes, so I won't be in for lunch.' He waited for her to ask why he was going to Carlington—she didn't. 'I could maybe have a bit of a lead as to what's been going on.' He had to try to chase some of the shadows out of her eyes even if there was not yet any room for optimism.

'Something that'll prove you're both innocent?'

He nodded. He did not point out that he couldn't hope to prove his own innocence, since he was guilty.

*   *   *

The traffic had been heavy and he did not reach Carlington until after two, having had a couple of sandwiches and a straight tonic at a pub after crossing the river. The centre of the straggling village was around a T-junction and a woman in the small general store gave him directions to the open prison. The five-minute drive took him past a garage, a butcher's, and a small council estate.

Protocol had to be observed. He should have

131

made a written request, countersigned by a superior, to speak to a prisoner. He explained to the assistant governor that he was engaged on an inquiry in which speed was of the essence which was why he'd short-circuited the regulations. He did hope that his action would not cause any misunderstanding or offence? He could, when he wished, adopt the trustworthy and very respectful, yet not deferential, manner of the good con-man. The assistant governor, normally a stickler for rules, said he quite understood.

'Very kind of you, sir. Now there's one more thing—if you could suggest which of the prisoners would be the most likely to be able to help?'

'You'd best have a word with Harmsworth, the chief officer. He's a good man; knows all the prisoners.'

Harmsworth had a moustache that would not have disgraced an RSM, but his manner was far from parade ground. He said, as he sat back in the chair in his small office: 'There's no doubt on that score. Fred Branson. He was Illmore's roomer for the last two months. But I give you due warning, Illmore was a real loner, so Branson may not be able to come up with anything . . . If you wait in one of the interview rooms, I'll winkle him out of wherever he's hidden himself—spends more energy on making certain he does nothing than if he did what he's meant to.'

'According to the information, Illmore's escape had a G code slapped on it.'

'So I heard.'

'That's a bit odd, isn't it, since he was only in for receiving?'

'I couldn't understand it, either. All right, he'd used a gun to escape, but guns aren't news any longer. Maybe it had something to do with the heavy metal who were along a few days before to question him.'

'Who were they?'

'I couldn't answer, except to say one was a detective chief superintendent and the other a detective-inspector.'

Stone whistled. 'That's strong enough for someone who's just emptied the Bank of England! Where were they from?'

'County HQ, as far as I know.'

'What did they want to question him about?'

'I've no idea ... Look, I'm sorry to push things along, but I've work that's waiting. So if you'll move into an interview room, I'll try to find Branson.'

A quarter of an hour later—he'd hidden himself well—Branson was shown into the small interview room that was painted in bright colours and on the walls of which hung a couple of attractive prints. He bore a likeness to a ferret. He was thin and sinewy, his hair prematurely white and his eyes dark and beady; his pointed nose seemed to twitch.

Stone passed a pack of Marlboro across the

plain wooden table. 'I'd welcome a chat about Roger Illmore.'

'Not found him, have you?' Branson sneered. 'Too bleeding smart for you.'

'Certainly for us country coppers.'

Branson was disappointed by the mild reaction. He opened the pack, tapped out a cigarette, asked for a light.

'You and he were cell-mates?'

'We call 'em rooms.'

'Sorry. Room-mates.'

'So what if we was?'

'You might be able to help me.'

Branson had trouble in explaining himself, lacking both vocabulary and the ability to express impressions, but eventually it became clear what he was trying to say. Illmore hadn't been so much unfriendly as coldly indifferent. Normally, the two men who shared a room talked to one another much of the time; half an hour could go by without Illmore's saying a single word. Even more extraordinary, he'd not been in the slightest interested in a copy of *Playboy* for which Branson had swapped a fortune in cigarettes...

Stone took a second pack of cigarettes from his coat pocket and fingered it. 'Seems like I'm out of luck, then—you're not going to be able to tell me anything more about him than I already know.'

'Depends what that is, don't it?' replied Branson, his beady eyes fixed on Stone's hand.

'He's thirty, was born and brought up in Liverpool, hasn't a fixed home, and this was his first time inside.'

'Some of that's cod's. He ain't no Liverpudlian, nor never was.'

Stone handed over the second pack.

It seemed that Illmore's self-imposed isolation hadn't been quite as complete as previously suggested. There had very occasionally been times when he'd been almost friendly and during one such time the subject of Liverpool had arisen. Branson, who knew Liverpool like the back of his hand, had become certain that Illmore didn't know Bootle from Broad Green...

'Did he talk with an accent?'

'He had a bit of a one, yeah, only it wasn't never grown on the Mersey.'

'Could you place where it did come from?'

'Never heard its like before.'

Stone wondered if Branson had learned anything more definite about Illmore's background? Had he ever talked about where he'd been living before his arrest? He hadn't. Had this really been his first time inside? So he'd claimed, but he'd shown no signs of stir fever and so it wouldn't be a surprise to learn he'd seen the inside of jail before. It just wasn't natural to be so calm...

The interview came to an end. Stone asked for the chief officer and was directed outside. He found Harmsworth by one of the carefully tended flowerbeds. 'There's just one more thing you could help me on. Illmore's down in the records as Liverpool born and bred, but according to Branson he hardly knew the place. What would you say?'

'The records aren't always right, are they? I mean, sometimes they've got to rely on the man himself for the info.'

'True enough. It does seem he didn't have a Liverpudlian accent. I asked Branson what it was if it wasn't scouse, but he couldn't answer.'

The chief officer twiddled the right-hand tip of his proud moustache. 'Funny you should mention that. When a new arrival books in, I have a bit of a chat to decide if he's likely to cause any trouble. There was something about Illmore that worried me, but I couldn't put a finger on what—and that's not being wise after the event. He was quiet, polite, obedient, but like a ... well, like a coiled spring. You need watching, I told myself. And so I took a special interest in him and that made me wonder where his accent came from. Never heard its like in thirty-one years and I've dealt with men from every part of the country. It got me thinking that maybe it was used to cover up another. But then I asked myself, why take the trouble? Never got an answer.'

When Stone drove off, his thoughts were confused. Illmore supposedly came from Liverpool, had been arrested on a receiving charge and sent to an open prison, in part because he'd no previous record. Yet a fellow prisoner was convinced he did not come from Liverpool; the chief officer believed it possible he'd developed one accent to cover up another—because it might hold a significance he had to hide; he'd no previous convictions, yet had settled into prison routine like a man who'd learned the hard way that to survive, he had to accept; he'd been convicted of nothing more serious than receiving, yet a detective chief superintendent and a detective-inspector had questioned him shortly before his escape; no more than a small-time criminal, he had organized, or had had organized on his behalf, a daring, armed escape … Contradictions galore. Stone decided to call in at county HQ to see if someone there could help him resolve any of them.

*   *   *

He spoke to a DC who had pointed ears.

'The Illmore case? I don't remember it off-hand, Sarge, so I'll have to check.'

Stone sat at the desk of a detective who was on sick leave. He did not have a long wait. The DC returned, dropped a file on the desk, pulled up another chair, opened the file. 'It was all straightforward enough. We'd had the whisper that a man called Harvey had been in on an armed robbery, so he was under surveillance. When the bust was made, Illmore was with him and in possession of a few thousand quid which could be traced back to the robbery.'

'Why wasn't Illmore charged with that?'

'There was the proof to tie in Harvey, but not Illmore. Receiving was the best we could manage.'

'Presumably, though, something big's cropped up since then?'

'Why d'you say that?'

'It was heavy metal that questioned him a few days before his escape from Torring Farm.'

'I'm not with you, Sarge.'

'The detective chief superintendent and detective inspector who visited him.'

'I never heard Mr Morley and Mr Price went along ... I'll just check.'

The DC was gone for only a couple of minutes. 'It wasn't either Mr Morley or Mr Price.'

'Then who were they?'

'You tell me.'

'Can I use the phone?' Stone telephoned Torring Farm and spoke to the assistant governor. Could he be kind enough to identify the two senior detectives who'd questioned Illmore? He did. Detective Chief Superintendent Rennick and Detective-Inspector Clarke of the Metropolitan Police.

He phoned New Scotland Yard. In which department did the DCS and the DI work? In the Anti-Terrorist group, south-east section.

Stone replaced the receiver, stared into space. Why should the head of an AT section have questioned Illmore unless it were suspected that either he was a terrorist or he was in a position to give valuable information about terrorism? No wonder a G code had been slapped on his escape.

CHAPTER FOURTEEN

The south-east section of the AT group worked from a divisional HQ in south London. Stone phoned and asked to speak to Detective-Inspector Clarke. He was put through to a detective-sergeant.

'What is it?'

The words had been curt, the tone curter. Stone was unsurprised. The men in specialist units soon donned a mantle of superiority. 'Will you give me what information you can on Roger Illmore?'

'Who?'

'He escaped from Torring Prison on the seventeenth of last month. Shortly before his escape, your guv'nor questioned him so I'm hoping someone will be able to fill in a few corners for me.'

'Hang on.'

He hung on, for quite a long time.

'The inquiries were of a routine nature.'

'In connection with what?'

'That doesn't concern you.'

'OK, so it's not my party.' Senior detectives disliked anyone who tried to butt into one of their cases; if the investigation ended in failure, they didn't want strangers to know this, if in success, they required all the credit. 'But you'll be able to tell me this much: is Illmore connected with terrorism?'

'No.'

'Then why was a G code issued after his escape?'

'Because he was armed.'

'That doesn't usually follow...'

'It did this time. And if you want to question the decisions of the DCS, do it direct.'

Stone replaced the receiver. He felt emotionally drained. The theory he'd been so laboriously building up had as much substance as a soap bubble.

*　　　*　　　*

The call came through after his fifth attempt to start the lawnmower and there seemed little left to do but curse all two-strokes. June called him in from the garden. 'It's Mr Abbott.'

'What can the great panjandrum want of little me?'

'I hope ... I hope it's not more trouble.'

'If it were, he'd have found someone else to deliver the news.' He smiled reassuringly at her, carried on through to the phone in the hall. 'Stone speaking, sir.'

'Why the devil can't you learn to obey an order? Who gave you the authority to question a prisoner at Torring Farm?'

'I went there on my own initiative.'

'Initiative? Goddamn insubordination! You were ordered to cease all work and go on leave. Do that.' Abbott cut the connection.

Stone replaced the receiver, turned to find June was standing in the doorway of the kitchen.

'It was more trouble, wasn't it?' she said in a defeated voice.

'No, it wasn't. But if you want to know what it was, I'm damned if I can answer.'

'But...'

'The message was, stay on leave and don't even think of work. *Voilà*, I'll do exactly as ordered.'

He returned outside and tackled the lawnmower for one last time before consigning it to the nearest junkyard. Life being full of unexpected twists, it now started at the first pull.

As he mowed the lawn, he considered the phone call. Normally, Abbott, who was a great believer in a chain of command because it preserved the majesty of rank, would never have made it, but would have detailed one of his juniors. The fact that he had, strongly suggested that he'd been ordered to do so. A

141

specialist unit could usually cross county boundaries and summon up enough clout to bring pressure even on to someone as high up in the pecking order as a DCS...

If AT were trying to have him gagged, it could only be because they were far more interested in Illmore than the detective-sergeant had let on; which meant Illmore was either suspected, or known, to be a terrorist; which meant that his theory was no soap bubble. Far from bringing his inquiries to a dead stop, he had to pursue them even harder.

*   *   *

It was a quarter to eight. 'I'll be off then,' Andrew said.

Stone stood. 'I'll just come out with you.'

June, who was knitting, looked up, her hands momentarily motionless. 'Where are you both going?'

'Andy's borrowing the car and I want to make certain before he goes that I haven't left some papers in it.'

She accepted the explanation and resumed knitting.

Outside, Andrew went over to the Escort and looked through the windows. 'I can't see any papers, Dad.'

'There aren't any. I wanted a word out of earshot of your mother. The less she has to worry about, the better ... Take things quietly.

Remember Confucius—Man with ears open and mouth shut learn more than man with ears shut and mouth open.'

'It would help if I knew what it is I'm trying to do.'

'Basically, it's to find out either where Joanna is or how to get hold of her. Anything after that will be a bonus.'

'Why exactly d'you need to talk to her?'

'For the moment, just accept that I do. There's nothing so convincing as ignorance. Remember, while you're trying to learn from Ogilvy, he may well be trying to do the same from you while appearing totally disinterested.'

'It's getting bloody complicated.'

'Your mother would probably say that the word "bloody" is totally unnecessary; for my money, something far stronger is totally appropriate ... Don't forget, there's been nothing in the media to connect our car with the fatal hit-and-run which means that he's no reason to couple you with that. So if, however obliquely, he starts talking about it, make a note of every word, every intonation, every pause, while all the time playing dumb.'

'I'm beginning to think that that's the only thing I'll be able to do efficiently.'

Stone smiled. 'If I didn't reckon you were right up to this, I wouldn't let you go.'

Andrew was gratified by the praise.

'Make it clear you're desperate to get in

touch with Joanna—which shouldn't take too much doing. If he says again that he's no idea where she and Betty are, ask for the parents' phone number so you can get on to them.'

*   *   *

Andrew left the car and crossed to the front door of Elsett Court, conscious of an inner feeling reminiscent of the times when he'd had good reason to fear the attention of pedagogic authority.

Miguel opened the door. 'Good afternoon, senhor,' he said in a heavily accented voice, as usual mixing up the times of day. 'Sorry, but the senhorita is not here.'

'No, I know. Is Mr Ogilvy in?'

'The senhor eats.'

'I'd like a word with him when he's finished, if that's possible.'

'Sure he will wish it. Enter, please. You is well?'

He was shown into the green room. He'd settled in one of the chairs and was leafing through a copy of *Country Life* when Miguel returned.

'The senhor eats a little more, then will talk. He asks, what you wish to drink?'

'May I have a gin and tonic, please?'

Fifteen minutes later, by which time he'd finished his drink, Ogilvy, wearing a lightweight suit which spelled Savile Row with

144

every nip and tuck, entered, a balloon glass in one hand, a cigar in the other. 'Evening, Andrew.'

Andrew came to his feet.

'I see your glass is empty. Would you like another?'

'No, thanks.'

Ogilvy sat. 'This taboo on drinking and driving is a restraint, isn't it? A reasonable intake of good alcohol is one of the necessaries of civilized life.' He sipped the cognac, to prove his point, drew on the cigar, let the rich smoke trickle out of his nostrils. 'Well, how's the world treating you?'

In the conversation which followed, there was no reference to the hit-and-run and had Andrew not been forewarned, it would not have occurred to him that he was being quizzed; even with that forewarning, he wasn't a hundred per cent certain that Ogilvy was not just proving himself an excellent host by interesting himself in his guest's interests. How was the computing going? Since his father was a policeman, had he considered working for the police since they must surely be using an increasing number of computers? Did he, as a matter of idle interest, have—through his father—a working knowledge of the law which would obviously be an advantage? Joanna did, but from the wrong side! She'd been charged with careless driving—it had taken expensive lawyers to get her off that—and twice with speeding . . . Cars seemed to encourage even the most respectable citizen to break the law, didn't they? Or was the law too restrictive? Could a law that was broken by the majority of persons be a good law? Who had the right to make a law which the majority defied? *Quis custodiet ipsos custodes*? Had Andrew ever been caught up in a motoring offence? No. If only so commendable a sense of restraint could be imparted to Joanna. Unless, of course, it was slightly easier for the family of a serving policeman to break the law with impunity . . .

Andrew said heatedly: 'If I tried to take advantage of Dad's position, he'd blow his stack.'

'I'm delighted to hear you say that. I've always thought that an Englishman is civilized because he respects the law, while a Continental isn't because he fights it.' He drained his glass. 'I'm going to indulge myself and have a second cognac. At my age, self-indulgence is one of the more fulfilling pleasures of life. Will you change your mind and have your glass refilled?'

'No, thanks.'

'A man of great will!'

Up yours, Andrew thought as he watched Ogilvy leave the room, trailing expensive smoke. When the other returned and settled, he said: 'Have you heard from Joanna?'

'Not a word. But then I wouldn't have expected any. Being a thoroughly modern woman, she's firmly of the opinion that communicating with elders is a bore. But you haven't heard either? That is rather surprising.'

'I do want to get in touch with her so I was wondering if you'd give me the telephone number of Betty's parents? They might know where she is right now.'

'As a matter of fact, I met a mutual friend only yesterday who said Bertrand and Fiona have decided to be away until the end of the month, so I'm afraid that they can't help. They do tend to take long holidays in the summer because he hates to be away in the autumn or winter since he's so keen on hunting and shooting.'

'Wouldn't there be someone in the house?'

'I don't think they have live-in servants—not since the couple who stole most of their silver.'

There seemed no point in staying any longer. Andrew, after thanking Ogilvy, left.

*   *   *

As Andrew climbed out of the car, Stone hurried out of the house. 'Did you have any luck?'

'I'm afraid I didn't get very far, Dad.'

'How far is that?'

Andrew slammed shut the driving door. 'He was friendly; even more so than last time. But when I asked for the phone number, he said there was no point in giving it because Betty's parents were away and wouldn't be back for some time and the house would be empty.'

'Did you ask for the address?'

'I didn't. I mean, if they're not there, what's the point?'

'To send a letter to Joanna in case she calls in there on her way back.'

'Shit! I never thought of that.'

'Not to worry. If the cover-up was deliberate, he'd have found some good reason for withholding the address as well ... Did he say anything that could help identify Betty's parents?'

'Only that their names are Bertrand and Fiona.'

'Sounds vaguely regimental—a second-class regiment.'

'I doubt they're second-class anything. Bertrand's mad keen on hunting and shooting.'

'I knew a publican who preferred beer to champagne, but kept a couple of hunters and rode to hounds twice a week ... Did Ogilvy try to quiz you over the hit-and-run?'

Andrew ran his fingers through his curly hair. 'I don't know if I was imagining things, but he asked me if I'd ever thought about working on computers in the police force and then got to pontificating about how the ordinary person can be as honest as the day's long, but put him behind the wheel of a car and he cheerfully breaks the law. That's no great

148

secret, but he started wondering if maybe I didn't have to worry about the traffic laws as much as other people because you were my dad … I know it doesn't sound much, only it could've been he was trying to find out about the hit-and-run without letting on. The big thing is, he was so friendly. Before that other time, if he met me he looked as if he was wondering where the anti-smell was.'

*　　　*　　　*

Stone, lying on his back, stared up at the ceiling which was faintly pricked out by the street light that filtered through the curtains and wished he could decide whether there was anything of significance in what Andrew had told him.

For a second time, Ogilvy had been unaccountably friendly. Yet few, least of all the rich, were consistent in their behaviour. And his sudden bonhomie might have nothing to do with his trying to draw out an unsuspecting Andrew. Business might have boomed that day and he'd made himself a few more thousands and so had returned home to dine and wine really well, whereupon major irritations became minor ones and minor ones disappeared … Yet Andrew thought there might well have been a significant undercurrent to all Ogilvy had said. Because there had been such, or because Andrew had been warned that there might be? …

149

'What's the matter, Gerry?'

June's words startled him. 'Nothing. Why?'

'Normally you fall asleep almost as soon as the light's put out, but you've been lying there, wide awake.'

'How do you know I have?'

'You've not been snoring.'

'It takes a wife to paint a husband with all his warts.'

She reached out and gripped his hand in hers.

*   *   *

The rain had not been forecast, but it bucketed down all the same. Those who had held their church fêtes the previous weekend breathed sighs of relief, those who had scheduled them for the coming one looked up at the grey-black clouds and wondered.

Stone was in the kitchen, washing up the breakfast things, when Andrew entered. ''Morning, Dad. Except it isn't.' He crossed to the working surface on which stood the coffee machine, checked that that was empty. 'Would you like another cuppa?'

'If one's going gash.'

'How's Mum?'

'More worried than ever because the morning's horoscope advises her to prepare for developments in the near future. She thinks they'll be unwelcome ones.'

'That could just about be right, couldn't it?'

'No more so than last year when she was led to expect a very pleasant surprise and Aunt Kathy rang to say she was coming to stay.'

Andrew filled the machine with water. 'Suppose ... Well, just suppose you can't find out anything more?'

'Unless you're a politician, never worry about the impossible.'

'I'm not still in shorts so that you have to hide the bad news.'

'But you still need to have it spelled out before you can bring yourself to accept it?'

'I ... I guess maybe.' He swung round. 'We've got to find out the truth.'

'Which is why earlier on I made a phone call to the research section at county HQ, asking them to draw up a profile on Ogilvy. And why in half an hour's time I'll be talking to the Masters of Foxhounds Association.'

'I don't see the point.'

'It's a real longshot. But Ogilvy told you Betty's father is a keen huntsman and from what you've gathered he's probably wealthy; wealthy hunters often end up as MFHs. I'm hoping to be able to persuade someone to track down all the Bertrands who have been in the recent past, or who are now, MFHs, and then with any luck I can, by elimination, find out which one is the father of Betty.'

'But there must be millions of names to check through.'

'Hundreds, probably. Which is why I'm going to have to talk very sweetly.'

Andrew put coffee into the machine, set it on the stove, lit the gas. He cut himself a doorstop of bread, buttered it, and smothered it in strawberry jam. He went to take a bite, stopped with the bread in front of his mouth. 'Give it straight, no hedging; what chance have you of ever proving the truth?'

'Very little,' Stone replied.

* * *

Stone was in the sitting-room, reading the paper, when Andrew entered.

'Dad, I've just remembered something which had completely slipped my mind until I switched on the computer and was about to start work. That night I went to pick up Joanna to go to the party, Mr Ogilvy happened to mention that Betty's parents lived in Shropshire.'

'Well remembered! Searching through the hunting records of one county is asking for a hell of a lot less than through forty-six— though I doubt one would need to linger long in Greater London or Manchester.'

* * *

Stone replaced the receiver. Luck was at last beginning to run with him. The Honourable

Bertrand Percival ffoulkes. The woman to whom he'd spoken had kindly pointed out that the surname was spelt with a small f.

He dialled the number she'd given him and wondered if there'd be an answer or if the ffoulkes really were on holiday...

'Yes?' asked a voice, filled with superior, tortured vowels.

'May I speak to Mrs ffoulkes, please?'

'Speaking.'

He knew the warm excitement that came from the possibility of having a longshot ride home a winner. 'My name's Detective-Sergeant Stone.'

She met that with disinterested silence.

'I'm trying to find out the present whereabouts of Miss Joanna Ogilvy.'

'Really.'

'I'm told you may be able to help me.'

'You have been incorrectly informed.'

'But you do have a daughter called Betty and she is a friend of Miss Ogilvy?'

'What if she is?'

'Then the two of them have driven up to the Highlands...'

'My daughter is in her flat in Chelsea.'

'Are you quite certain of that?'

'My good man, I spoke to her over the telephone less than an hour ago.'

It was a long, long time since he had been called 'My good man'.

CHAPTER FIFTEEN

One swallow didn't make a summer; one lie didn't make a man guilty. Yet after all his years in the force, Stone reckoned to be able to identify the stink of crime even when it was drenched with the scent of roses...

He telephoned Essex county HQ and asked if the gold Fiesta, stolen on the night Illmore had escaped, had been recovered. It had not.

Illmore's need to organize the armed escape from prison had almost certainly been triggered by the visit of the two senior detectives from the AT unit—that visit had shown him he was in imminent danger of being positively identified as a terrorist and therefore he had to get out of the country immediately. Since he could be certain all ports and airports would be very closely watched from the moment the escape was known, he would have planned to leave by boat, sailing out of some isolated, half-hidden creek. But when the BMW crashed, he was sufficiently badly injured for the original plan to have been wrecked, probably because by the time he could move, it was too late. So he'd been faced with the necessity of reaching a hiding place where he could hole up until he'd recovered sufficiently to organize a second escape. He'd stolen the Fiesta and, because he was a man of fanatical determination, had managed to overcome his injuries sufficiently to drive south. On arrival at Elsett Court, there had been the problem of the Fiesta. Were it seen, it would betray him, so it had to be hidden or disposed of in a way that ensured it would not be found before he'd left the country. What safer place than one of the garages at Elsett Court where there could be no chance of its being seen accidentally by someone who would appreciate its significance?...

Stone went upstairs. Andrew was seated in front of his computer, tapping in instructions which caused the display on the VDU to change rapidly. Stone settled on the end of the unmade bed and waited until the columns of words and figures became static, then said: 'You know the lay-out at Elsett Court pretty well, don't you?'

'Parts of it.' Andrew swung round in the office chair to face his father.

'What outbuildings are there?'

'There's a courtyard at the back of the house and on the far side of this there's a range of buildings which originally were the stables and the grooms' and gardeners' accommodation. Some of the stables have been turned into garages; as far as I know, all the rooms above are empty or used for storage space.'

'So how many garages are there?'

'Mr Ogilvy keeps his Bentley and Volvo in the biggest, Joanna has her Porsche next to it, and the Portuguese couple have an old banger in another—there must be three more, though I haven't actually counted them.'

'Are they lockable?'

'Joanna's certainly is, but then hers and Ogilvy's have up-and-over metal doors, worked electronically. The others have ordinary wooden doors, but I can't say if they can be locked. Why the interest?'

'Just a casual thought.'

Stone returned downstairs and went through the kitchen into the garden, to stand in the sunshine. Find the car and his theories could become facts. The only way of being certain the Fiesta was in one of the garages at Elsett Court was to obtain a search warrant and look, but no magistrate would issue one to a detective-sergeant unless presented with sufficient evidence to make it reasonably certain that it was there ...

*   *   *

Stone was not a proud man, but he did see himself as privileged to be in the front line in the fight against disaster. Without him and his companions, law and order would be overwhelmed because man's vices would, if given the chance, always overcome his virtues. And because he believed he served a cause, he had never been tempted to cross the line between right and wrong, not even on the day

156

he had been offered five thousand pounds to look the other way and there had not been the slightest risk in his doing so. Which explained why it was not until 6.17 that evening that it occurred to him that the lack of a search warrant did not of necessity preclude a search of the garages at Elsett Court. At 6.18 he dismissed as ridiculous any thought of an illegal search. At 7.33 he wondered if the garages had windows and if they were wired to the house's alarm system. At 8.10 he angrily reminded himself that the end never could justify the means if the means were illegal...

'Gerry.'

He looked across the sitting-room at June, now knitting the back of the sweater.

'How much longer are they going to make you stay on leave?'

'There's no saying.' There was, of course. The forensic laboratory had named the eleventh as the earliest possible date on which they'd be able to deliver a report on the paint. So any day after Tuesday, that report could arrive at divisional HQ and make it certain that the paint found on the footrest of the motorbike had come from the Escort.

'They can't go on like this, leaving us not knowing. It's not fair.' Her voice rose.

He crossed to sit on the arm of her chair and hug her. He could feel her trembling and he guessed that her mind was filled with the nightmare of son and husband in prison...

It was a coward's defence to hold that the end could never justify the means if the means were illegal.

*   *   *

June, an intermittent churchgoer, was attending morning service. Had he believed in the efficacy of prayer, Stone would have joined her, but his experience of the harsher sides of life had convinced him that a man was better advised to rely on himself. He went upstairs to find Andrew still in bed. 'If you're not careful, you'll take root.'

'It is Sunday, Dad.'

He crossed to the window, drew the curtains, and watched their neighbour back his Golf GTi on to the road with a careless disregard for other vehicles. 'I'm going to ask some questions. After you've answered them forget I ever asked 'em. Understood?'

'Not really. Why...'

'No why's.' Stone turned. 'Can one approach the courtyard at Elsett Court from the east?'

'If that's from the lane which borders their land, sure you can. There's even a track which is probably what the tradesmen used in the old days.'

'Are there gates to the courtyard?'

Andrew's answers created a picture in Stone's mind. The courtyard was formed by the north side of the house, the stable block, and two high brick walls. There was a gateway in the east wall and the gates were not always closed during the day, even though they were operated by remote control from the cars—Joanna was usually to blame, regarding any rule, obligation or duty as something to be either ignored or flouted. Ogilvy kept his two cars in the right-hand garage, Joanna her Porsche in the next one, and the Portuguese their ancient and rusty banger in the third. There were no obvious signs of alarms in the courtyard or in Joanna's garage.

'What do you know about the alarm system in the house?'

'Only what Joanna's told me—and what I've learned when ... Well, you know.'

Movement and heat sensors, pressure pads, contact points, all connected to a computer that had been programmed to filter out false alarms; a stand-by generator automatically starting and cutting in if the outside power lines were cut; a radio telephone to contact the operations room at county HQ if the telephone line was cut. Even a top professional would think thrice before he tackled a house that well defended. So if the same level of defences had been extended to the garages ...

'What are you thinking of doing, Dad?'

Committing an anglicized version of hara-kiri, he thought.

CHAPTER SIXTEEN

June, her expression strained, faced Stone across the sitting-room. 'It's after midnight. Where on earth can you be thinking of going now?'

'There's something I have to do.'

'What d'you mean, "something". Why won't you put a name to it?'

'Because it's better if you don't know.'

'My God, how can you be so blind? You can really believe it's easier for me not to understand what's going on? Can't you realize that that only makes it worse?' She stared at him, her large brown eyes filled with fear. 'You're about to do something dangerous, aren't you?'

'There's no danger.' He hoped he sounded more sincere to her than he did to himself.

'Please, I beg you, don't do it.'

'I must.'

'Why?'

'To find out if I'm right.'

'And proving you're right is all that matters?'

'You don't understand...'

'Of course I don't, because I'm only a wife and a mother.' She moved suddenly, crossed to the door, went out and slammed the door shut behind her.

Fear could scramble her mind until she could no longer think or speak rationally. He pictured her in their bedroom, no longer dry-eyed, besieged by nightmares. He wanted to go upstairs and comfort her, but knew that if he did he would lose his resolve.

He went through to the garden and round to the car. On the front passenger seat was a holdall and he opened this to check the contents, knowing he had already done so just before dark. Years of experience gained from his side of the fence and the unguarded conversations or bitter comments from those who worked on the other side had taught him what every intending burglar needed. Plastic torch with bowl hooded by masking tape; gloves, jeans, sweater, plimsolls, and ski mask, all bought from multiple stores; a length of clothes line, knotted at regular intervals; a hook, made from two lengths of wood nailed together ... All things which, with the exception of the batteries and nails, could be burned after use. Every contact left a trace, but a short-lived one if the receiving article were reduced to ashes. He patted the right-hand pocket of the jeans to feel the set of skeleton keys that looked like small dentist's probes, which had been given to him some years previously, probably in a moment of angry exasperation because it had been the third time he'd arrested the man.

The journey to the woods just east of Elsett

Court took over twenty minutes—the nearer he drew, the slower he drove. It was no easy thing to betray his instincts, upbringing, and training.

A wide ride led to a clearing, hidden from the road, that was a favoured spot for couples requiring privacy. To his relief, love seemed temporarily to be on the back burner because no other cars were there. He'd removed the bulb from the rooflight, so the car remained in darkness when he opened the driving door. He changed into the clothes from the holdall.

The moon had not risen and within the woods it was almost pitch black. He switched on the torch, whose beam had been reduced by the masking tape to a spotlight only inches across, and made his way across the clearing and down the ride on the far side to the edge of the woods. He stared across the countryside—only one light was directly visible, a long way from where Elsett Court was.

He crossed the first field, down to grazing, without the aid of his torch and reached a five-bar gate. In the next field there were sounds which suggested a herd of cows. Only recently, he'd read that surprised cows were angry cows and were to be more feared than angry bulls. As he climbed the gate, he wondered how one could persuade them that one came in peace.

A well-maintained yew hedge marked the house's grounds. He found a gateway and passed through and now, ahead of him, a wall of blackness, delineated by the star-studded sky, showed him where the house and outbuildings were, though it was not yet possible to differentiate between them. A grass path that initially ran alongside the hedge eventually looped round to bring him to a brick wall. This was, provided he'd maintained his sense of direction—a quick check on the Pole Star showed him he had—the rear wall of the stable/garage block. Andrew had said that the gates were on the east side of the courtyard; he carefully made his way to the wall on the west side.

A successful (up to a point) burglar had once confided in him that the secret of a good break-in was always to expect, and therefore plan for, the worst. He was having to expect the best—that all the alarm defences pointed inwards and none, at least in the courtyard, outwards—an assumption that seemed justified when he remembered that when Andrew left the house by the back door, only the alarm to that and the courtyard gates had needed to be switched off.

By standing on tiptoe, he was just able to hook his improvised wooden grappling-iron over the top of the brick wall. By pulling down on the knotted cord that was made fast to it, he made certain it was as secure as possible, then he climbed up on to the top of the wall, a surprisingly difficult task, despite the knots and short distance involved, because of the thinness of the cord.

He sat astride the wall and waited, ready to retreat at the first suggestion of an alarm. There was none. He hauled up the cord, dropped it into the courtyard. Rule number two. Before you go in, always make certain you can get out.

He climbed down to the cobbles, which caused him to move very slowly and carefully, and went round the edge of the courtyard because if there were, after all, sensors guarding areas of the outside of the house, these would probably he mounted on the wall opposite to it and therefore he needed to keep within their dead ground. He came to a set of wooden doors. This must be the last of the unused garages. He found the handle and turned it, but the doors were locked. Standing in front of the lock, to shield it from the house, he switched on the torch. The appearance of the keyhole and surrounding woodwork suggested the lock had not been altered in many years. That was the good news. The bad news was that he quickly learned it needed more skill than it seemed he possessed to make the twirlers twirl. He used each skeleton key in turn, altering its depth and angle, and the force with which he worked it, and the tumblers remained immovable. Silently cursing his lack of skill, convinced it spelled failure, in frustration he jabbed a key sideways. The tumblers turned. It seemed that locks had something in common with two-stroke lawnmowers.

He opened the door. He could just make out that there was a car inside, but it was impossible to ascertain any details. He went inside, shut the door, and switched on the torch. A gold-coloured Fiesta with a registration number which identified it as the car stolen from the farm near Brentwood.

CHAPTER SEVENTEEN

On Tuesday morning, a telephone call ordered Stone to divisional HQ to speak to the DI. Kemp, seated behind his desk, handed him three sheets of paper held together by a paperclip. 'These arrived addressed to the CID; inside the envelope was a note naming you as the requestor.'

It was the profile on Ogilvy which he had asked Research to produce.

'Aren't you going to read it?'

He couldn't make out what the DI's aggressive manner portended. 'I don't want to interrupt your work . . .'

'You've interrupted it. Sit down and read.'

He moved a chair away from the wall, sat. There was a short headnote. Very few details of the subject's early life seemed to be available.

Richard Steven Ogilvy. Forty-seven-years-old. Born in Ballycurry, Northern Ireland. Father, a clerk with the local authority. Educated in local schools. Moved to London when he was sixteen and started work as an office boy in a firm of commodity brokers. At the age of twenty-three founded an importing and exporting company. Despite cyclical trading conditions, firm had always prospered. His reputation was of a skilful, straightforward businessman whose great strength was that he knew when not to take a risk. There had been rumours that his company would go public, but this had never happened. The company now specialized—though not exclusively—in exporting luxury leather work to the United States and importing from there luxury seafood, both from and to Spain as well as to the UK. The report ended with a string of figures, virtually meaningless to Stone since he was no accountant.

On the face of things, he thought, the report sketched in the kind of success story which had universal appeal because it seemed to prove that anyone with an idea, self-confidence, and sufficient determination, could tread the path from rags to riches. But was this story quite so straightforward as that? Whilst men did rise from humble beginnings to riches and positions of power, their journeys were seldom quick, yet Ogilvy had gone from office boy to company chairman in seven or eight years.

Where had the money or the influential help come from which had enabled him to make so quick a climb from so low a base? Could the answer have something to do with the fact he had been born in Northern Ireland?

Kemp said: 'When did you ask Research for this profile?'

'On Friday.'

'Which was after you were ordered to drop all the work you were handling and to go on leave?'

'Yes, sir.'

'Why are you so interested in Ogilvy that you disobey orders? Because you think he's connected with the hit-and-run?'

'Yes.'

'That would appear to be very unlikely.'

'Yet it's almost certainly true.'

'Are you suggesting he was driving the car involved?'

'No.'

'Then what makes you believe he can have any connection with the crash?'

'Because I think he's involved with terrorism and that the crash was deliberately engineered in order to conceal the connection.'

'In effect, you're now saying that he murdered Hutton?'

'Hutton was murdered because of him.'

'By whom?'

'I've no idea.'

'If I hadn't worked with you for some years,

I'd probably say you were trying to take me for a fool.'

'If he has no connection with terrorism, why should he be hiding the Fiesta that was stolen after a known terrorist escaped from prison?'

'What terrorist? What prison?'

'Roger Illmore escaped from Torring Farm on the seventeenth of last month. The change-over car, a BMW, crashed and at least one of the occupants was injured. A gold-coloured Ford Fiesta was stolen from a farm close to the site of the crash—there's no proof Illmore stole the Fiesta, but it's a hundred to one he did.'

'How do you know Ogilvy is hiding that Fiesta?'

'It's in one of his garages.'

'How can you be certain?'

'I chanced to see it there.'

'You just chanced to see it there!' Kemp repeated, with heavy sarcasm. 'You broke into the garage.'

There was a long silence.

'A man in your position is only going to act that bloody stupidly if he's trying to protect himself or someone he loves. Which confirms it *was* your son who was driving your car which hit Steven Hutton.'

'It wasn't my car and he wasn't driving.'

Kemp fiddled with the corner of a file. After a while, he looked up. 'Terrorists aren't held in open prisons.'

'At the time of his capture and trial, Illmore

168

wasn't known to be a terrorist. But later, the possibility came to light and that's why a DCS and DI from an AT unit questioned him in prison. And it was that visit which told him he was suspected and had to escape before suspicion turned into proof.'

'How do you know two officers from AT questioned him?'

'One of the prison staff told me.'

'For a man on leave, you appear to have been busy! Have you spoken to someone in AT to confirm that Illmore is a suspected terrorist?'

'I had a word with a detective-sergeant who said that he definitely wasn't.'

Kemp's expression became quizzical. 'And that doesn't knock the bottom out of your theories?'

'I reckoned it did, yes, until Mr Abbott phoned and blasted me for making unauthorized inquiries and ordered me to drop the case. I reckoned it was so out of line for him to deal directly with a detective-sergeant that he must have been leaned on by someone on high. That wouldn't happen unless my inquiries were beginning to hit a sensitive spot, like threatening to expose negligence on the part of AT.'

'I see.' Kemp thought for a moment. 'I'm going to make a couple of phone calls now. Report back here in an hour's time.'

Stone left.

Kemp telephoned county HQ and spoke to Abbott. 'I've just been informed, sir, that you telephoned Detective-Sergeant Stone at his home and admonished him for disobeying orders and prohibited him from continuing his investigations into the escape of Illmore from Torring Farm. Is that correct?'

Abbott, who had a bully's instincts, said angrily: 'That's no concern of yours.'

'With respect, it is. If true, there's been a breakdown of command. Both admonition and prohibition should have passed through me as Stone's divisional DI.'

'In a matter like this, the normal chain of command is immaterial.'

'I'd have thought otherwise. Stone is under suspicion of trying to pervert the course of justice. Surely in such circumstances it's doubly essential to observe all correct forms?'

'Look here, Kemp, I'm not used to having a junior officer trying to tell me my job.'

'And I, sir, am not used to having my authority undermined. The circumstances being what they appear to be, I would have been justified in making a formal complaint, but I thought it probably best to have a word with you informally to see if things could be sorted out without creating too much hassle upstairs.'

Abbott ceased to be so authoritative. 'All I

was trying to do was to keep the matter under close wraps.'

'Then you believe that had I known about it, I would have broadcast it?'

'Of course not. Why are you being so goddamn sensitive?'

Kemp pressed home his advantage. 'Because I'm responsible for everyone under my command and therefore am entitled to know what affects them.'

'And in the normal course of events, naturally I'd have left you to deal with the matter.'

'What's abnormal?'

'I was asked—ordered would be a better word—to deal with the matter as discreetly as possible...' He tailed off into silence.

'Who gave the order—a DCS in AT?'

'Higher ... It's obviously politically very sensitive, Kemp, so for heaven's sake don't do anything to bring it out into the open. Just dampen everything right down.'

'Why is it so sensitive?'

'I've no idea. And that is of no more concern to you than it is to me.'

As a consequence of the call, they disliked each other a little more.

Kemp dialled a London number and asked for Detective-Superintendent Brabazon. 'Do me a favour, will you, Ted?'

'Not if I can avoid it.'

'You do owe me one.'

171

'I've a feeling that this is going to prove to be the most expensive debt I've ever incurred. What do you want?'

'Information concerning a case that's with AT, south-east. Why are they so steamed up about Roger Illmore that they've tried to put the chokers on the details of his escape from Torring Farm open prison?'

*   *   *

When Brabazon phoned back, he said by way of greeting: 'You bastard! You damned near landed me in the shit! Why didn't you say that the name of Illmore was a red rag to a bull?'

'Because I didn't know that.'

'Then next time do your homework before you involve someone else ... Illmore was picked up because he was found in the company of Harvey who was suspected of armed robbery. It could be proved that some of the money in his possession came from that robbery so he collected eighteen months. Later, AT were involved in another case which provided a lead straight through to Harvey and named him as a fundraiser for an active wing of the IRA and suggested he'd been in touch with an IRA member who was an expert in explosives and rocketry, and also made it clear that if AT had been even half awake, they'd have discovered these facts long before. Naturally, AT's done its damnedest to defend its backside while it's been busting a collective gut trying to discover if Illmore was the explosive and rocketry expert. He virtually answered that question for them when he escaped, but that left them with even more egg on their faces. So when a certain Detective-Sergeant Stone turned up, threatening to introduce a little light on to the scene, they took very distinct um.'

It had developed into the kind of situation which any ambitious detective-inspector fervently hoped to avoid.

*　　*　　*

Stone returned to divisional HQ. Kemp pointed to the chair in front of the desk, waited until Stone was seated and said: 'It can't be proved that Illmore's a terrorist, but there's reason to suspect he belongs to the IRA and is an expert in explosives and rocketry. So now you're going to tell me what you know, holding back nothing.'

'I have, sir.'

'You have not begun to explain how the hit-and-run is tied in with Illmore.' Kemp waited, but when there was no comment, he continued. 'Do I have to underline the consequences of failing to recapture Illmore if he is the man he now appears to be; to remind you of all the hundreds of totally innocent people who have been killed or bloodily maimed by bombs? Are you ready to see their numbers increased?'

'That's still only a possibility.'

'You know it's a probability.'

'At the moment, all I can be certain of is that I'm more concerned about people I do know than people I don't.'

'That's one hell of a selfish attitude.'

'Realistic. The death of a friend is always more traumatic than the deaths of even a hundred strangers ... But suppose I agree. Just how unselfish are you prepared to be?'

'What do you mean by that?'

'Will you trade your honour as a policeman for the lives of these as yet unidentified victims?'

'Are you asking me if I'll agree to take no action on whatever you tell me?'

'Yes.'

'You know where to put the boot in, don't you?'

'I've had to learn the hard way.'

'Including when you broke into Ogilvy's place ... It's odd, isn't it, that although some of us regard our job as a trust, there are others who sneer at so archaic an attitude yet are none the worse detectives because of that? The smartest man I ever knew in our job took bribes up to the day he retired ... All right. You've jumped down from your ivory perch, I'll jump down from mine. I give you my word that anything you tell me now will never be used by me against you or your son. What I cannot and will not promise, however, is to destroy any evidence already on record or to ignore any that comes to hand from other sources.'

'How to eat your cake and have it.' For a while, Stone was silent, then he succinctly detailed events of the night of the seventeenth and his conclusions concerning them.

Kemp said slowly: 'Illmore's escape was time-critical in order to ensure he was out of the country before anyone in AT could respond. When the crash incapacitated him for long enough for those plans to go for a burton, he was left with only one option—to find a safe billet where he could recover and hide until the heat was off. He chose Ogilvy's place.

'When Andrew left the house, he ran into Illmore who'd just arrived. Illmore assumed he was an intending burglar and only learned later that he'd been a departing Romeo. That meant he was in danger because Andrew and Joanna must exchange details of an extraordinary night and you, a detective, would probably learn at least enough to excite your interest and probably suspicion ... Something had to be done to prevent your becoming dangerously interested. So Joanna was shipped off and Andrew was implicated in a hit-and-run because this must leave you crazy with worry and little time for anything else.'

'So now?'

'Isn't that obvious? We apply for a search warrant of Ogilvy's place on your evidence which will be backed by me. AT may have put out the stoppers on Illmore, but they can't prevent us investigating a case concerning a stolen car.'

*   *   *

Ogilvy met them in the hall. ''Evening. It is Andrew's father, isn't it?' The use of the third person could have been offensive, but he came forward with outstretched hand and a smile. After shaking hands, he looked inquiringly at Kemp. 'And you are Detective-Inspector Hemp?'

'Kemp.'

'Miguel usually manages to get things wrong. It's an old Portuguese custom . . . Come along into the other room and have a drink before you tell me what's brought you here.'

'Thanks, but we won't,' replied Kemp, with formal politeness. 'We're here, Mr Ogilvy, with a request.'

'Requests are easily made; it's their implementation which can be difficult. However, if I can help in any way, I most certainly will.'

'I've information that there may be a stolen car somewhere on the premises and I'd like your permission to look for it.' It was policy to try to gain voluntary cooperation even when in

176

possession of a search warrant—if granted, it became much more difficult for defending counsel to shout foul.

'It's very unreliable information. I can't believe that the ancient Vauxhall of Miguel's was ever stolen—surely the modern thief wants something very much smarter?'

'His is the only car on the premises?'

'There are my two, of course, but they were bought through dealers so respectable that it's probably akin to blasphemy to suggest any funny business. My daughter's Porsche is away at the moment.'

'There is no gold-coloured Ford Fiesta in one of the garages?'

'There is not.'

'Would you object to our making certain of that?'

'Of course not.'

His ready, smiling agreement told them that their search was going to prove to be a waste of time.

Fifteen minutes later, they drove away. As they neared the road, Kemp said: 'Didn't anyone ever warn you about markers left in a lock?'

CHAPTER EIGHTEEN

Stone parked next to the Superintendent's Rover. 'Next?' said Kemp.

'The Fiesta bloody well was there.'

'I'm not arguing about that. I'm asking what you reckon our next move should be?'

'God knows!'

'Then I suggest we both need a drink.'

It was not often that Kemp chose to drink with other members of CID, preferring a hands-apart style of command. They walked out of the car park and down the road to the Four Feathers, sometimes described as the spirituous home of the men of F division.

They settled at one of the tables, not far from the dartboard. Kemp produced a pack of cheroots and lit one with the care of an occasional smoker. 'The moment they discovered someone had broken into the garage, but nothing was stolen and there were no signs of forced entry anywhere else, they judged you were responsible. Which meant they had to move really quickly. The Fiesta will have gone in one direction and Illmore, sufficiently recovered, in another. It no longer matters if or when the Fiesta's found because Illmore will have fled the country rather than search for another hiding-place. A regular port or airport would still have been too risky, but it's not difficult to organize a small boat to France or Ireland ... So accept that Illmore's out of the country and the Fiesta's no longer important. What have we left? Ogilvy. Who might be persuaded to talk, but only if he's put under sufficient pressure. Can we prove that Illmore was in Elsett Court, making Ogilvy guilty of harbouring an escaped prisoner?'

'Andy can't swear that the man who zapped him was Illmore. The fact that that man had a bloody face confirms but doesn't prove that he was. That weekend the two Portuguese were away. It can't have been difficult in a house that size to fit Illmore up with a hiding-place and to make certain that when the servants returned, they didn't catch sight of him. They're foreigners, less able to judge when circumstances are unusual.'

'You don't think there's much to be gained from questioning them?'

'Probably nothing.'

'There must be a promising lead somewhere.'

'There's only one I can think of right now.'

'Which is?'

'Joanna. The odds have to be that she came face to face with Illmore the night he arrived. She could identify him.'

'Where is she?'

'According to Ogilvy, on holiday with Betty ffoulkes somewhere in the Highlands, but Mrs ffoulkes says her daughter is in London.'

'Can you make an inspired guess where Joanna is right now?'

'Andy can't, which means I certainly can't.'

'Which turns that lead into a dead end.' Kemp tapped the ash off the end of his cheroot. He spoke in a low, angry voice. 'Out there is a man who sees it as his mission in life to murder; if we could catch him and ship him back to jail, lives would be saved. Ogilvy might be able to help us catch him. But the law says we are not allowed to use physical or psychological force to make Ogilvy, or any other witness, give evidence, however vital that may be, because that would be to betray our conception of justice. And it makes no difference if failure to secure the evidence will result in the deaths of innocent victims. They must be allowed to die in the name of democratic justice ... So we have to wait until the day the telly shows us bodies blasted by a bomb and then we'll know that those bodies are bodies because we weren't allowed to do our job as efficiently as we wanted to ...'

*   *   *

June dished two eggs and two rashers of bacon and put the plate on the kitchen table in front of Stone.

'Thanks, love,' he said. 'By the way, aren't you having lunch with Stephanie today?'

'I don't think I'll go.'

'Why not?'

'I don't feel like it.'

'It would do you a world of good to get away.'

'And leave you having to get lunch?'

'I reckon I'm just about capable of putting something in the microwave to keep Andy and me from starving until you return.'

The coffee-maker hissed. She went over to the cooker and turned off the gas ring. 'Gerry ... What's happening? With you and Andy and the accident?'

'At the moment, nothing.' He ground pepper on to the eggs.

'Don't try to hide the truth. I'm not afraid.' She was terrified. 'Love, nothing's happening because nothing can until the lab makes its report.'

'And then?'

'We've got to wait and see what then.' He looked down at the *Daily Mail* by the side of his plate. The date was the eleventh. The earliest day on which the forensic laboratory had said it could make its report on the paint...

'You must have some idea,' she persisted, knowing in her heart that if truthful he could only confirm disaster and driven by some strange destroying urge to hear him say so.

'There's a chance the lab will say they can't provide the definitive proof the court must have.'

'But suppose...'

'Supposing is bad for the health and should carry a government warning.'

'Why won't you be serious?'

'Because it's not a serious world. If it were, the government would be on the stage and we would live in Cockaigne.'

She said: 'You're a fool and I love you for it.'

'I admire your good taste.'

'Don't ever dislike yourself, will you?' Her tone had become almost light.

As he ate, he wondered not for the first time why he continued to shield her from the truth? Because he was a coward when it came to facing her despair or because he still had an instinctive, irrational hope that somehow things would be all right in the end? The cavalry didn't always arrive in time. But how did one stop oneself listening for their hoofbeats?

As she washed up, chatting inconsequentially, he finished the eggs and bacon, ate two slices of toast with homemade marmalade, and drank a second cup of coffee.

She upended a saucepan on the draining-board, untied her apron and hung this up. 'I think you're right, Gerry, and it would be good for me to have lunch with Stephanie, so if you really don't mind, I'll go up and change and then leave. I'd like to see as much of her as possible.'

'So would I.'

182

'God, you men!' As she passed him on the way to the door, she ran her fingers through his hair.

He skimmed through the paper. International bickering, EEC bureaucratic incompetence and intransigence, murder, rape, fraud ... Man as he was, is, and always will be ... He heard June start downstairs and went out into the hall. 'You look like spring.'

'Thank you, Sergeant Galahad.' The smile she gave him was both spring and summer. 'When Andy gets up, tell him there are clean clothes, ironed, on the bed in the spare room.'

'I'll also inform him that in my day only the lame and the sick remained in bed after seven-fifteen.'

'Your mother said you were always impossible to get out of bed.'

'Mothers have inconvenient memories. Give Stephanie my regards.'

'Not your love?'

'Do I dare?'

'All the time she lives in Sussex and we live in Kent, you dare.'

There was a touch of careless gaiety in her manner. He smiled at her, she laughed which made him do the same, and neither of them really knew what they were laughing about. She linked her arm with his and they went out together, shuffling sideways through the doorway and finding that hilarious. She kissed him before she settled behind the wheel of the

Escort.

He walked out on to the pavement and waved her on to the road. Back in the house, he stacked his breakfast things on the right-hand draining-board, then picked up the paper and went through to the sitting-room where he read what previously he'd only skimmed. He had just finished the sporting news when there were the sounds of movements from upstairs. He went through to the hall. 'Andy,' he shouted.

Andrew, tousle-haired, appeared at the head of the stairs.

'There are clean clothes for you in the spare room.'

'Thanks.' He disappeared down the corridor, to reappear within seconds. 'Hey, can I borrow the car this morning?'

'You're out of luck. Your mother booked first.'

'But she won't be all that long, will she?'

'She's having lunch with an old schoolfriend who's recently and very unexpectedly produced another baby; the combination of fifth-form memories and a squalling brat will probably ensure that she's there until long after tea-time.'

'Don't you like babies, Dad?'

'Not until they're twenty-one and have joined the human race.'

It suddenly and simultaneously occurred to them that Andrew was not yet twenty-one and it was his actions which had landed them in the

184

position in which they now found themselves. As Stone tried to find something to say that would repair his gaffe, Andrew retreated out of sight.

Stone went through to the kitchen and out to the garden, sat on the swing-hammock. The lawn was recently mown, the flowerbeds were weedfree, the tomatoes in the greenhouse had been side-budded ... He was like a newly retired man, wondering how on earth to occupy his time...

He just heard the doorbell chime. Experience suggested Andrew would wait to find out if someone else would go to the door, so he made his way back into the house. The caller was a uniform PC. For a moment, he couldn't place the other, then he remembered. ''Morning, Pete. What's brought you here?' Even as he put the question, he was certain of the answer. A summons to divisional HQ because the report from the forensic lab had arrived.

'Sarge, there's ... there's been ...'

In a flash of shocked recognition, he realized that only one thing could produce this embarrassment. 'What's happened?' he demanded, his voice twisted with fear.

'There's been a bit of an accident. Not really an accident...'

'For Christ's sake, man, what's happened?'

'It seems, like, there was a bomb in your car.'

The words seemed to come from an infinite

distance and it took him an infinite time to understand them. When he did, he wanted to shout that it was impossible. 'How is she?'

'Sorry, can't say. I was just told to come and tell you your wife was being taken to the Thomas Quenton Hospital.'

'She's alive, then?'

'Like I said, I don't know anything more.' He spoke almost sharply, trying to cover his own feelings.

Stone turned, raced back to the front door, stopped as he realized he'd no car. 'Wait and drive us there.'

He went inside. The hall had not changed, the small mirror near the telephone showed that he had not changed, yet all had shattered. He remembered being told by one grieving relative that the cruellest thing was to discover how the world beyond was totally unconscious of the tragedy. He told himself that people lived through bombings, but remembered those when only bits and pieces had been available for the funeral.

He hurried upstairs. 'Andy.'

Andrew, hair still more wild than curly, appeared in the doorway of his bedroom.

'June's injured and is being taken to hospital.'

'Mum's hurt! Oh God! Not badly?'

'The PC doesn't know.'

'What happened?'

'The car was bombed.'

'Jesus! She can't be hurt badly. Not badly.'

They raced downstairs.

A second PC was at the wheel of the patrol car. 'Sorry about what's happened, Sarge,' he muttered. He started the engine and drove off as soon as they had settled in the back.

'Why?' said Andrew, in a voice which quavered. 'Why should anyone want to hurt her like that?'

Incredibly, only now did Stone ask himself the same question. The answer was obvious. He had been the target; whoever had set the bomb had not known that he was off-duty and therefore quite likely not to be the first to drive.

They cut through the back streets to reach the main road to the coast, which for a while ran parallel with the motorway and then bore off to the east. The fifteen-year-old hospital was on a rise and in view some time before they turned into a side road. Stone and Andrew stared at it as if the sheer intensity of their gaze could find the answer to their desperate question.

The patrol car drew up outside the main entrance. 'I hope the missus is all right,' the observer said.

'Thanks,' Stone replied briefly.

He led the way inside and over to the reception desk. 'Mrs Stone. How is she?'

The young woman, who had been faced by so much heartache that she'd learned to keep it at a distance, said with professional calm: 'I'll

187

see what I can find out.'

She made three calls on the internal telephone, looked up as she replaced the receiver. 'Mrs Stone has been taken into the operating theatre. If you go along to waiting area four and give your name to the receptionist there, a doctor will have a word with you ... That's in the east wing. Along this passage to the lift, get out on the third floor and turn right.'

His mind was too scrambled consciously to memorize the instructions, yet he led the way without hesitation. There was a large, well-illuminated square, around which were bench seats; in the centre was a work station at which a middle-aged woman sat. He gave his name.

'If you'll sit down, Mr Stone, I'll see that someone has a word with you as soon as that's possible.'

He and Andrew sat and stared into space, living with their private nightmares.

*   *   *

A middle-aged man dressed in green theatre cap and gown, face mask about his neck, had a brief word with the receptionist and then walked across. 'Mr Stone. I'm Dr Fieldmaster.'

They stood. Time almost stopped.

'I'm happy to say that none of your wife's injuries is critical. She has suffered shrapnel wounds which have led to some internal damage, burns, a broken leg, and her hearing has been badly impaired. We've operated successfully on the wounds. Full hearing should return of its own accord in time. She will be in considerable discomfort for a while, but there's every reason to think she'll make a full recovery.'

CHAPTER NINETEEN

Kemp stood by the burned-out wreck of the Escort, looked at the shattered shop windows, and wondered how there could have been only one casualty apart from June Stone.

'The DCS is here,' said Wearing.

He turned to see Abbott ducking under the tape which had been strung across the road. In the strange way in which a mind could work at an unusual moment, it occurred to him that the Detective Chief Superintendent needed either a new suit or to let out the buttons of the one he was wearing.

Abbott walked up. 'Is that right that Mrs Stone isn't in danger?'

'The hospital calls her condition comfortable. Which, for my money, is an odd way of describing someone who's been blown up.'

'And there was only one other casualty?'

189

'A twenty-five-year-old woman who was cut by flying glass.'

'It's a bloody miracle!'

'Partly thanks to PC Willis. He was off duty and walking along the far side of the road when the bomb went off. He dragged Mrs Stone out of the car a second before it became engulfed in flames.'

'Have you any idea why the car was bombed?'

'A very good idea.'

'Which is?'

'It's a bit of a long story, better told at the station. I've everything on hold here, waiting for AT to come and advise, so we might as well go there now.'

* * *

Abbott, his plump face expressing irritation, said to Kemp, who sat behind his desk: 'You've given me a damned sight more assumptions than facts.'

'They were assumptions. This bombing turns them into facts.'

'Only if you assume a direct connection between it and Illmore.'

'Not very hard to make.'

'Isn't it? When you understand the full consequences of making that assumption?'

'Which are that AT have to admit they've made a complete BU of things, initiate a

190

priority search for Illmore, and back a full investigation into Ogilvy's background.'

'They won't like that.'

'I don't like having the wife of my sergeant blown up.'

'What I'm really saying is, it'll have to be done tactfully. Don't forget, the order to gag Stone came from high up.'

'Meet altitude with altitude. Get the Chief Constable to do the talking.'

Abbott scratched his neck. 'When I was a DI, I thought that all my seniors were wimps. Now I'm a DCS, I know that all my DIs are hotheads.'

Kemp was surprised by this display of self-deprecating humour.

*　　*　　*

Kemp would have scorned any suggestion that he was something of a father-figure, yet he always made a point of doing everything he could for any of those in his command who ran into trouble. He was waiting in his car when Stone returned home in the hired Fiesta. 'How's the wife?' he called out, as he stepped out on to the pavement.

'Considering everything, fine,' Stone replied.

'What's the prognosis?'

'With any luck, a complete recovery.'

'I'm very glad to hear that ... Would you like

to ask me in?'

'Sorry I haven't suggested it. I'm not thinking straight at the moment.'

'No one would expect you to be.'

They walked up to the front door, which Stone unlocked, then went in and through to the sitting-room. 'You'll have a drink?'

'In the circumstances, I most certainly will.'

'There's beer, gin, whisky, or some sherry which June says is really only good enough for cooking.'

'In the face of that recommendation, I'll settle for a gin and tonic, thanks.'

Stone poured out the drinks in the larder, returned to the sitting-room. Kemp raised his glass. 'To a complete, speedy recovery.' He drank, put his glass down on the occasional table by his side. He asked permission to smoke, lit a cheroot. 'AT's pro tem. report is that your wife owes her life to inefficiency. The bomb was placed under the back seat of the car instead of the front and the contact trigger wasn't set properly and so didn't operate as it was meant to. This suggests that either Illmore isn't the expert he's said to be or the bomb was planted by someone else. Since logically Illmore will have fled the country, we're working to the second premise.

'The remains of the car have been taken away for a detailed examination. The experts seem confident that eventually they'll know the type of bomb used and hope that that could provide a lead. Meanwhile, everyone with any known connection with terrorism is being turned over and a very solid reward is out for a good grass.

'All possible sources of information here and in Ulster will be tapped by AT, in cooperation with the security forces. Ogilvy will be questioned by us while his background will be investigated by AT who've become expert in sniffing out murky loyalties.'

Stone said drily: 'It sounds as if AT have finally decided they're fighting on the same side as us.'

'The Chief Constable made certain they forgot about their own skins and started worrying about other people's.' Kemp tapped his cheroot over a glass ashtray. 'The first question which needs to be answered is, did they try to kill you to keep your mouth shut or in revenge for causing them so much trouble? Is there anything more you know but have not told me because it would be dangerous to your son or you?'

'You know as much as I do.'

'I was hoping you'd been holding something back ... Were you here all last night?'

'Yes.'

'No alarms—no cars driving off at three in the morning?'

'June and I went to bed early and slept right through.'

'Just for once, a touch of insomnia might

have been useful ... We'll have a word with the neighbours, of course, but I'm less than hopeful that they'll have heard or seen anything useful.'

Stone stood. 'Can I give you a refill?'

'Thanks.' Kemp held out his glass. 'A little less gin, if I may.'

When Stone returned, he placed a bowl of crisps on the table beside Kemp. Kemp picked up a crisp. 'According to Marie, every one of these puts up my blood pressure by a millibar, or however they measure such things.' He ate that crisp, helped himself to another. 'That's why I'm not allowed them at home.'

Stone thought that is was difficult to visualize the Detective-Inspector's being denied anything he wanted.

'I suppose it has to be admitted that right now the only fruitful lead we have is Ogilvy. How well do you know him?'

'Yesterday was the first time I've met him to speak to.'

'How do you read him on that very brief acquaintance?'

'Clever, smart, prepared to play the game politely unless and until he wants something; then he'll play it any way that's likely to be successful.'

'I'd go along with all that ... Do you think your son would be able to add anything?'

'I don't really know, except to say that Andy's rather wary of him. But if one has any sense, one is a little wary of the father of the girl one's bonking.'

'OK, he's smart and he's tough. So he's not going to crumple just because we ask him a load of questions which make it obvious we suspect him. Then unless we can get hold of something definite, he's unlikely to become a source of information. Have you had any fresh ideas on finding his daughter?'

'There's no room to have any.'

Kemp took a last draw on the cheroot, stubbed it out. 'It looks like we're going to need a bucket of luck to get anywhere.' He stood. 'But maybe we had our full ration of that when Illmore didn't stop around long enough to plant the bomb himself.'

*   *   *

Wearing, seated in the front passenger seat of the CID Montego, looked through the windscreen at Elsett Court as they drove towards the raised, circular flowerbed. 'It's a lovely place. Jacobean, by the looks of it.'

Kemp was surprised to discover that he'd not wondered in what period the house had been built. One of the troubles of police work was that it trimmed one's range of interests.

'I've always had a dream of owning a place like this. It's lucky that dreams don't cost.'

Miguel let them in and showed them into the green sitting-room; he said, in his fractured

195

English, that the senhor would be with them very soon. In fact, Ogilvy, accompanied by another man noticeably taller than he, arrived only after several minutes.

Ogilvy did not apologize for the delay. 'This is Mr Naylor. I decided, after receiving your request for an interview, that it might well be advisable for my solicitor to be present.' His manner was authoritative, but not belligerent.

Naylor had a long, thin, humourless face which went well with his precise, at times pedantic, speech and behaviour. 'Good morning, gentlemen. You will, of course, understand that the sole reason I am here is because there may be a legal point which Mr Ogilvy will wish to have clarified.'

Kemp said drily: 'It's a wish we're familiar with.'

Ogilvy said: 'Do sit down, Inspector. And if you like to have that chair...' He turned briefly to Wearing, before speaking to Kemp once more. 'Well—how can I help you?'

'I imagine you will have heard about the bomb incident in town yesterday morning?'

'A shocking affair, made doubly shocking by the fact that the victim is the mother of a friend of my daughter's. I've never met Mrs Stone, but naturally I immediately got in touch with the hospital to learn how she was ... You may find this naïve, Inspector, but I am truly astonished that such a thing could happen in Peteringham. Have you the slightest idea what

196

possible motive there could be for so appalling a crime?'

'Her husband was the target, not her. And the motive for his murder stems from one of the cases he's recently been investigating, which is why we're here now.'

Naylor said: 'Do you have proof that Mr Stone was the intended victim?'

'Hard proof, no.'

Naylor, who'd settled a director's case on his lap, wrote in the notebook he'd placed on its lid.

Kemp addressed Ogilvy once more. 'We've been checking the cases DC Stone has recently handled and last Tuesday—'

'One moment,' interrupted Naylor. 'Last Tuesday you and Detective-Sergeant Stone came here in pursuance of certain investigations. Was Mr Stone on duty at that time?'

'Since he accompanied me—'

'Was he not officially on leave?'

'That makes no difference.'

'You don't think it might have rendered your visit an unorthodox one?'

'A detective on leave does not cease to be a detective.'

'A detective without the proper authorization does.'

'He had all the authorization he needed,' snapped Kemp. 'Mr Ogilvy, while we were here, we asked you about a gold Ford Fiesta—'

'Inspector,' said Naylor, 'did you at that time have in your possession a search warrant naming these premises?'

'Yes.'

'Yet you did not serve it?'

'It was unnecessary. Mr Ogilvy willingly agreed to our looking through the garages.'

'By not serving it, you avoided having to disclose the information on which it was based. What was that information?'

'That it was possible a gold-coloured Fiesta was on the premises.'

'What was peculiar about this car?'

'It was stolen.'

'When?'

'On the night of the seventeenth of July.'

'In other words, you were accusing Mr Ogilvy of having harboured a stolen car for more than three weeks?'

'I made no accusation.'

'You will be conversant with accusation by inference. Had you found this car in one of Mr Ogilvy's garages, what would you have said and done?'

'Since I didn't, that's a hypothetical question.'

'To which you would far prefer not to give a hypothetical answer? From where did your information come which led you to imagine there might be a stolen car in one of the garages?'

'I am not prepared to identify the source.'

'Was it Detective-Sergeant Stone?'

Kemp was silent.

'Why should Detective-Sergeant Stone believe a stolen car was present when, to Mr Ogilvy's knowledge, he has never set foot in the house or its curtilage?'

'I have not said that he was the source of the information.'

'Are you prepared to say he was not?'

'Mr Naylor, I'm here to ask Mr Ogilvy a few questions, not to be subjected to what virtually amounts to a cross-examination—'

'I am certain you would find a true cross-examination far more difficult to answer. After all, were we in court, you would have to try to explain why you were so willing to act on fallacious information which had been obtained dishonestly by a member of your staff who was on leave as an alternative to being suspended.'

Kemp shrugged his shoulders in a gesture both of anger and resignation. 'One last question, Mr Ogilvy. Would you object to telling us where your daughter is?'

'Not at all. Unfortunately, I have no idea. She left to go on holiday with a friend and I've not heard from her since.'

'Was the friend Miss Betty ffoulkes?'

Naylor quickly said: 'What is the relevance of that question?'

'Perhaps I'd like to ask Miss Ogilvy why her father says she's on holiday in the Highlands with Betty ffoulkes while Mrs ffoulkes says her daughter has not left London.'

Ogilvy turned his head so that it was briefly hidden from the two detectives.

'A man of your experience has not yet learned that the modern daughter often expresses her independence by deliberately confusing her parents about her plans?'

'You sound as if you have a difficult teenage daughter.'

Six minutes later, as they drove away from the circular flowerbed, Kemp allowed his anger to surface. 'How did that smart-tongued bastard of a lawyer learn Stone was virtually suspended?'

'It's amazing what they manage to winkle out,' said Wearing stolidly. 'Still, you shoved one up his nose! If you ask me, he's got a daughter who leads him a real dance.'

'I hope it's the bloody post-horn gallop.'

CHAPTER TWENTY

There was a seldom used conference room on the top floor of divisional HQ. Some said it looked more like an undertaker's parlour, but that was being over-critical of the framed photographs of past divisional superintendents. It was also to ignore the view which stretched beyond the town to the surrounding countryside and the hills.

Abbott, being the senior officer present, was in the chair. He was quite a good chairman, thanks in part to his wish always to find the easiest way out of a problem. On his right was a detective-superintendent from AT. A large, florid-faced man, frequently overbearing in manner, he made little effort to hide his opinion of country policemen. Accompanying him was a detective-sergeant who had the smooth but superior manner of a born administrator. Seated opposite the two from AT was Kemp.

Coffee was brought in by a cadet. After one mouthful, the detective-superintendent said he imagined no one would object if he smoked and lit a cigarette before Abbott had time to object.

'Shall we start?' said Abbott, irritated by such bad manners, but not prepared to make an issue of them. 'The first question to be considered obviously is, how certain can we be sure that Illmore is a terrorist?'

'Quite certain,' said the detective-superintendent.

A certainty only recently acquired, Kemp thought ironically.

'He is identified as a member of the IRA and an expert in explosives and missiles.'

Abbott turned to Kemp. 'In the light of that, what can you tell us?'

Kemp fingered the single sheet of paper in

front of himself, but did not bother to consult it. 'We know that the bomb on Stone's car was fixed in the wrong place if the intention was to kill the driver and that the detonating switch was inexpertly set. These facts suggest the bomber was inexperienced which confirms he was not Illmore.

'Our inquiries have been proceeding along two lines—trying to prove the bombing is directly connected with Illmore and uncovering evidence which will identify the bomber. As to the first, we've checked back on all cases Stone has handled in the past twelve months and have come up with nothing other than the episode concerning the gold-coloured Ford Fiesta which he claims was in Ogilvy's garage. As to the second, we've questioned everyone who lives in Stone's street, we've tapped in to a large number of grassers, we've posted a very solid reward for information, and have come up with nothing.'

'Because this job was done by a small, relatively inexperienced unit that was brought in for the one job and then rushed out,' said the detective-superintendent, believing it necessary to explain the obvious.

'So it's going to be very difficult to get a lead on them?' asked Abbott.

'You can't make bricks without clay.'

'Unfortunately not ... Does anyone mind if I open a window as it is becoming rather smoky in here?' He stood, went over to a window and opened it, returned to his seat.

The detective-superintendent stubbed out one cigarette, lit another.

'I suggest we look at things from a slightly different viewpoint,' said Abbott, staring with dislike at the newly lit cigarette. 'If one accepts Stone's evidence—' he paused; he hoped he never heard all the facts—'then Illmore, injured when the BMW crashed, managed to drive the Fiesta from Brentwood to Elsett Court. He then stayed there, recovering, until he was suddenly forced to move on. This would mean that Mr Ogilvy, at the very least, must be a strong supporter of the IRA; more likely, an active member. Yet his lifestyle hardly supports that assumption, does it?'

Kemp answered. 'His lifestyle may not do so, sir, but the fact is that when I interviewed him, he had a mouthpiece who blocked almost every question I asked. That suggests he's a good reason to be afraid, which wouldn't be the case if he had nothing to do with terrorism.'

'A very negative assumption,' said the detective-superintendent.

'Two negatives make a positive.'

Abbott hastened to smooth waters which might become ruffled. 'Let's move on. Steve—' Abbott used christian names when speaking to those who were only one rank junior to his; a democratic gesture—'can you fill us in more fully on Ogilvy's background than the profile which we already have and which you must

203

have seen?'

The detective-superintendent nodded at his detective-sergeant, who brought out two sheets of paper from a folder. 'We've traced out what we can at short notice. Despite the name, he comes from a Catholic family who, prior to Cromwell's time, were fairly large landowners. However, following the 1641 revolt, crushed so brutally, the Ogilvys lost most of their land. Probably they were also involved in the 1689 revolt, because by the end of the century they were reduced to a life of penny-pinching. A good breeding ground for long-lasting resentment.'

'Facts, not opinions,' growled the detective-superintendent.

'Facts don't start again until 1920 when Ogilvy's father was involved in a nasty little incident with the Black and Tans and was wounded and taken prisoner. When finally released, he was in poor health, both physically and mentally. Once the new government was installed, he was given employment as a clerk in a local government office—probably as a reward for past services rather than because he was qualified for the work involved.

'Richard Ogilvy lived at home in Ballycurry until he was sixteen, then moved to London where he started work as an office boy in a firm of commodity brokers. After seven to eight years, he left that job, although highly regarded and marked out for rapid promotion, and founded his own import/export company.'

'Which would have called for a considerable sum of money,' said Abbott.

'I was about to come to that.' Despite the difference in rank, the detective-sergeant did not add a 'sir'. 'We've looked at what he was probably earning when he was employed and what it would have cost him to live and it's quite clear he could not have saved anything like enough to form the company and sit things out until it was in profit. Since his family continued to live in very ordinary circumstances, it's certain that the necessary capital did not come from them. We've nothing to suggest where it *did* come from.'

Several seconds passed before Abbott realized that the detective-sergeant had come to the end of his report. 'What's your reading of all that?'

'Ogilvy is a quartermaster mole,' said the detective-superintendent.

'I imagine I understand the expression, though I've not met it before.'

'Born into a family that had reason to hate the English, he probably saw himself as heir to all the injustices his country had ever suffered,' said the detective-sergeant, allowing his imagination a little more rein than his superior would probably have liked. 'Someone in the shadows must have been keeping an eye on him, marking him as sharp, intelligent, and sufficiently committed to become an underground worker. He was sent to London where his task was to become the epitome of a successful English businessman, a pillar of social and financial respectability. A camouflage that would enable him to mix with people whose information could be useful, to arrange the purchase and shipment of arms, and to launder hot money.'

Abbott said: 'There's an objection to that scenario. The IRA would have invested years of effort and considerable financial resources in him and that means they'd do everything possible to avoid having his true position revealed. Would Illmore even have known his true calling, let alone have deliberately risked compromising it?'

'Yes, if two conditions pertain. One, Illmore is high enough up in the organization to be party to its most secure secrets; two, the possibility of his capture would potentially be even more damaging than the exposure of Ogilvy.'

'It's difficult to think how that could be.'

'Knowing that Illmore was an expert in explosives and missiles, we checked nationwide for activity in these fields which might indicate an IRA interest. There was none. We then contacted Interpol and asked them to check worldwide. They came back with details of a theft in the States which occurred two months ago. Three LAGSSAM launchers and twelve rockets were stolen from the Tumbleweed

Proving Grounds. This information had not been disseminated this side of the Atlantic because all the available evidence suggested the theft had been carried out by, or on behalf of, Central or South American interests.'

'And because they didn't want to make any more public than necessary the fact that they'd been caught with their trousers down?' suggested Kemp.

The two from AT stared at him with open dislike.

Abbott hastily said: 'And you reckon Illmore is in some way connected with that theft?'

The detective-superintendent answered. 'First, I'll return to the original question. Would even the possession of these missiles and launchers warrant the risk of exposing Ogilvy?' He leaned forward until his stomach was up against the table; his voice ceased to hold the hint of contemptuous superiority that it had previously contained. 'I've had a talk with a man who's up in these sort of things and who knows the LAGSSAMS. They're small enough to be handled by one man and fired from the shoulder. They have laser sights and the missile locks on to the beam which means that all the firer had to do is keep the laser on target and he doesn't have to worry about aim-off. A raw recruit, shown what to switch on and pull, can make a hundred per cent kills. They're short-range weapons and effective only with targets travelling at under two-fifty to three-hundred knots, but against helicopters they're deadly. In Northern Ireland the troops rely on helicopters. Twelve missiles wouldn't ground every helicopter over there, an unlimited number would.

'Since a raw recruit can fire them with great effect, why is a man of Illmore's qualifications so essential? There's only one possible answer to that, isn't there? His task is to strip launchers and missiles down to their last nut and bolt in order to organize the manufacture of that unlimited number.'

'Jesus!' exclaimed Abbott. 'With a prize like that, the possibility of compromising Ogilvy's position becomes small beer.'

'Exactly.'

'Would you expect Illmore to be in Ireland now?'

'Almost certainly.'

'And the launchers and missiles?'

'Both the Irish and Ulster authorities report that there's nothing to suggest they are. That could mean everything or nothing since the operation will be under maximum security.'

'But we have to presume it's too late to contain the problem?'

'I'm afraid so.'

'Then God help the troops over there.'

'Two Amens to that.'

'What about Ogilvy?' asked Kemp.

They turned and stared at him.

'It's surely ten to one that he organized the shipment of the launchers and missiles to Ireland. We can put pressure on him to give us details.'

'Can we?' said Abbott. 'Remembering that when you tried to question him, he retreated behind a mouthpiece. Short of thumbscrews, there's no obvious way of getting him talking.'

'Then use thumbscrews.'

'Don't be ridiculous!' Abbott snapped.

'He's our one lead that's left. Are you saying that it's more important we observe all the rules and regulations, even though he's a terrorist, than that we try to save the lives of God knows how many ordinary, decent people?'

'You obviously need to be reminded that you're a policeman.'

'For once, I wish I could forget the fact.'

CHAPTER TWENTY-ONE

They sat at one of the tables in the pub, Kemp on one side, Stone on the other. Beyond them, four men were having a cheerfully loud game of darts; behind them, two off-duty PCs—who from time to time looked curiously at the two detectives since rumour had placed Stone in disgrace—swapped impossible boasts with the middle-aged landlady who laughed at all the right moments.

'There must be some way of getting at him,' said Stone.

'Thumbscrews have been ruled out . . . Drink up and I'll get the other half.'

Stone drained his glass and passed it over. Kemp had the glasses refilled, returned to the table. 'If you can't solve your problems, drown 'em.'

They drank. Stone said: 'Guv, where does all this leave me?'

'Precisely where you were.'

'Yet but for Andy and me, none of this would have come to light.'

'You're expecting a quid pro quo? Haven't you yet served long enough to learn that however much quid you give, you'll get bloody little quo in return?'

Stone fiddled with the handle of the glass. 'All right, so I don't get awarded the police medal. But where do *you* stand in things?'

'In relation to you? Where I promised you I'd stand. What you told me in confidence will remain confidential.'

'But if the lab report identifies my car, what will you do?'

'Whatever the law demands.'

'Even though you'd have acted as I have if you'd been in my shoes?'

'We're forbidden that sort of emotional relief valve.'

                    *   *   *

'What did Mr Kemp say, Dad?' Andrew asked.

'That nothing's changed.'

'But ... but that's impossible.'

'As far as the law's concerned, things are straightforward. If I tried to hide the evidence of the crash, I'm guilty of attempting to pervert the course of justice.'

'After all you've done? They wouldn't know anything but for you.'

'That doesn't alter my crime. In fact, even if we could prove you weren't driving the car at the time of the crash, it wouldn't make a scrap of difference.'

'You've got to be fooling me. If I'm not guilty, there's no way anyone can say you were trying to hide my guilt.'

'Under English law, one can be found guilty of attempting the impossible.'

'Then the law's crazy.'

'Only partially. It's a question of intention ... Feel like a drink?'

'I need a big one after that.'

After pouring out the drinks, Stone led the way into the dining-room.

'Dad,' said Andrew, 'just how gloomy are things?'

'Like a traditional pea-souper. Since the paint on the motorbike came from our Escort, it's difficult to see how the laboratory can miss.'

'So when ... when will you know for sure?'

'They told me that the earliest they could come up with their report would be three days ago. It could happen any time.'

'And then we're both for the chop?'

'I don't know so much. I've been thinking that maybe a really smart lawyer could do something for you. As I see things, a lot's going to depend on whether your case is heard before mine on the grounds that they are totally separate offences, or whether the court decides to lump 'em together since one grew out of the other. If you're tried separately and first, then my attempting to hide the damage to the car won't necessarily be in evidence. In which case, you'll be faced with having to make a decision. Do you stand silent and leave the prosecution to make all the running, knowing that their case isn't watertight because they have to prove not only it was our car but that you were driving it at the time; yet also accepting that if they can show a good enough case, you'll be very hard pushed to rebut it? Or do you tell the truth from the beginning, a man with a snow-white conscience, hoping the jury will accept it? The trouble with that is, juries are so unpredictable. Mention the Mickey Mouse masks and they might believe you, admire your imagination, or be incensed that you should think them such burkes as ever to believe you.'

'It all sounds kind of tricky.'

'Of course. If the law weren't extremely

tricky, how would lawyers feed their life-style?'

'So that's me. What about you?'

'No difficult decisions to make. When the lab identifies the paint, I'm for the chop. Which means a solid dose of imprisonment in order to satisfy the British public who become very sanctimonious when a policeman proves he's only human.'

'I'll tell them you did it entirely for my sake.'

'And feed their sense of outrage? A father who dares to place his son before his duty? No wonder we lost the Empire.'

* * *

Stone began to understand that man really could fear something, yet as time stretched out the fear, reach the point where he longed for it actually to happen to bring an end to the waiting.

He looked across the kitchen table at the calendar which hung on one of the cupboard doors. The eighteenth. How many more days? ... He heard the rattle of the front-door flap, went through to the hall to find four letters in the letter-box; two for him—bills—one for June, and one for Andrew.

He went upstairs, to find Andrew awake, but still in bed. 'You'll make the *Guinness Book of Records* for the greatest number of hours in the horizontal position.'

'I read only yesterday that it's good to keep

213

the legs up because that puts less strain on the heart.'

'Yours must feel as frisky as a pup.' He went over to the window and drew the curtains, returned to the bed and dropped the letter on to it. 'This arrived in the morning's post.'

'Thanks, Dad.' Andrew picked up the envelope, took one look at the writing, and began to blush.

A crazy thought swept into Stone's mind. 'Who's that from?'

*   *   *

Kemp sat back in his chair and stared at Stone, who stood in front of the desk. 'Did you read the letter?'

'No. Andy assured me that there's nothing in it to give even a hint of where she's staying.'

'It would have been much better if you'd checked that that's so.'

'From the way he was acting, he reckoned I'd be shocked by some of the things she'd written.'

Kemp made a snorting sound. 'Damned if I ever had the luck to receive that kind of a letter.' He picked up the envelope. 'Why the hell is it that whenever it's important to be able to read a postmark, the bloody thing's smudged?'

'Sod's Law.'

'Let's hope the post office can decipher it. If

214

we can get her to identify a photograph of Illmore, we'll have a sword to hang over Ogilvy's head. It's my experience that however committed to a cause a man is, when he's faced with the choice of losing his comfortable life-style or his commitment, it's the first which wins hands down.'

'I suppose we ought to let AT know what's happened?'

'And have them barge in and try to take over? If this proves a solid lead, you need to grab full credit for providing it.'

*　　　*　　　*

The sorting office in Peteringham phoned through at six-fifteen that evening. They were reasonably confident the letter had been posted in Seascale; however, it was possible that the postmark was Seaford or, less likely, Seaton.

'We'll go for broke,' said Kemp. 'I'll phone Cumbria and tell 'em the postmark is Seascale and will they give you every possible help in tracing Joanna Ogilvy.'

*　　　*　　　*

Stone stared through the windscreen at the rain which, blown by a westerly wind, slanted heavily. 'What a day!'

The detective-constable who was driving laughed. 'You southerners are all bloody soft!

215

This is good bracing weather.'

'It is supposed to be summer, you know.'

'And didn't we see the sun the week before last!'

They passed a line of shops and then turned into a small parking space to the side of a stone-built house. 'I warned Sammy we'd be along about now, so he should be around. He's young, but smartish.'

They left the car and hurried through the rain to the doorway at the side of the house. Beyond was a small room equipped as an office in which a PC was working at some papers at a table which did duty as a desk.

'Hi, Sammy, so how's the world?' said the DC.

'Like always. Too much work for too little pay.' The PC stood.

'You want to get married, mate, instead of playing the field, and find out what life's like when you've really something to moan about ... This is DS Gerry Stone, up from the south; took one look at our lovely weather and wanted to go straight back there.'

Stone shook hands. The DC sat on the edge of the table. 'So. Have you anything for us?'

The PC said: 'Only negatives so far, but I'm still trying ... D'you feel like a cuppa?'

They said they would like some coffee. He left the room, returned within the minute. 'The kettle's on.' He moved a chair. 'There you are, Sarge.' He went round the table and sat. 'I've been on to the local postmen, but none of 'em remembers a letter addressed to Joanna Ogilvy. I've spoken to shopkeepers, taxi-drivers, and hotels, all without any joy. Sorry, but that's how things are at the moment.'

'It's about what I expected,' said Stone. 'After all, her aim and object is to keep out of sight.'

'Then you've a problem,' said the DC, neatly transferring that problem off his own shoulders.

'There are one or two things we have to go on, though. She's from serious money, which means it's odds on that she's staying with money. So we're probably looking for a family which lives in style. Are there many big places around here?'

The PC answered. 'Depends what you mean. It's not a part of the country for estates. But I'd swap bank accounts with some of the farmers who shout poverty as they drive past in their Mercs.'

'Could you draw up a list of wealthy people in the area?'

'That's a bit of a tall order.'

'Yeah, I know. But the letter was posted in Seascale which means there's a good chance the family lives closer to here than the next post office or postbox that would give a different postmark. So you can cut the area down.'

'Don't forget that this is tourist country. They could have driven out for the day and only posted here by chance.'

'Which would mean we hadn't a hope ... Let's say we're going to get lucky and they do live locally.'

'I'll do what I can, then, Sarge. There is one thing and that's have a word with 'em up at the golf club. Most of the local money's there at some time or other.'

*　　*　　*

The PC picked up a handwritten list from the table and passed it across. 'I've kept it strictly local, Sarge, like you said.'

'Thanks a lot. I hope it wasn't too much of a sweat?' Stone briefly studied the names and addresses. 'Is it OK if I use your phone to work through all of them?'

'Sure. That is, if you don't mind signing a chitty to say that that's what you've done. They watch the phone bill here like I've a girlfriend in New York ... Then I'll leave you to it. I'm trying to obtain a witness statement from an old farmer who doesn't want to give it and who'll rush out to the hills if he sees me coming. Stubborn old bastard!' He left.

Stone had dialled the first number on the list, found it engaged, and replaced the receiver when the PC looked round the door. 'Nearly forgot. Ted, the golf pro, mentioned the Havertons and there might be something in it. The husband's so bad at golf he can't even slice well, but being rich he's forever buying different clubs because he thinks that'll turn him into a Faldo. Ted says that a few days ago Haverton came into the shop with a young woman who was obviously staying with him.'

'Did you get a description?'

'Hot blue eyes, wavy brown hair, and the kind of figure that makes a man breathe faster.'

'So far, so good. Do you know the Havertons?'

'Only by sight. They say Mrs Haverton is a bit scatterbrained ... Just thought I'd mention it.' He nodded, left.

Stone looked through the list for the Havertons' number, dialled it. A woman answered. 'Mrs Haverton?'

'She's out. Can't say when she'll be back.'

Her Cumberland accent was so strong, he could only understand her with difficulty. 'Perhaps you can tell me if Miss Joanna Ogilvy is staying in the house?'

'She's out as well.'

Luck, he thought, with a rush of excitement, had returned.

CHAPTER TWENTY-TWO

Sweetwater Hall was large, bluntly shaped and stone-built; it looked as if it would shrug aside the next two hundred years as easily as it had

219

the last. Just visible from the drive was the tarn which gave it its name.

The sturdy wooden door, which had never been treated with any preservative and was weathered grey, was opened by a small, overdressed woman. 'Mrs Haverton?' Stone asked.

'Yes?'

He introduced himself and the DC, asked if Joanna had returned.

'I'm afraid she hasn't. She drove over to Keswick to see friends—or did she say they were distant relatives? I can't remember.' She spoke with resignation, as if she often couldn't remember.

'Then you won't have any idea of when she'll be back?'

'No ... Yes. What I mean is, we're going out for drinks and she'll want to get ready for that, so she can't be long, can she? Would you like to wait?'

The hall was two floors high, hung with tapestries, and watched over by two full suits of armour; one expected to hear madrigals from the half-landing. The sitting-room was huge and filled with a mixture of modern and antique furniture which went strangely well together; through the windows the tarn was visible beyond a well-kept lawn.

Mrs Haverton sat on a velvet-covered armchair. She cleared her throat. 'I do hope nothing's wrong? Joanna's father has not had

220

an accident?'

'As far as I know, Mr Ogilvy is fine,' Stone answered.

'Thank goodness. Accidents happen so suddenly, don't they? And if he'd been injured, Joanna wouldn't have been able to go on the trip she's so looking forward to; or at least I think she is—it's difficult sometimes to understand the modern generation, isn't it? She's very fond of her father. Not, of course, that they don't have their little tiffs. What parent and child doesn't? And to tell the truth, Joanna can be a little headstrong. If things don't go exactly as she wants them to ... When she came up here, she really was ... Not because she didn't like being here, but because it wasn't she who had arranged the visit. When her father rang, he naturally asked how she was and I had to tell him that she was in a bit of a difficult mood. But then later, after they'd had a chat and he'd told her what he'd arranged, she became her usual charming self. Things were made very difficult for both of them when her mother died. And since then, Richard has rather spoiled her ... Although all children are spoiled these days, aren't they?'

Lulled by the flow of words, it took Stone a couple of seconds to realize that an answer was needed. 'Compared to the old days, I suppose they are.'

'When I was young, you wouldn't have found a father doing what he's done just to cheer up her bad temper. Don't you agree?'

'I'm not certain what he has done.'

'Arranged for her to go on this cruise. At least, it's not really a cruise, not in the sense one used to mean. And because this kind of trip is so popular these days—apparently it's been booked up for months because there are always people who don't like masses of other passengers—someone had to have her booking cancelled, or altered, or something. I've always said, one person's good luck is another's bad luck ... I do envy her. I keep trying to persuade my husband to travel more, but he won't. He says that there's nowhere like home. Well, that's true, but it makes it seem all fresh when one returns from other places. And she'll be seeing where the Armada sailed from. One of the turning-points of history. And "Not a drum was heard, not a funeral note"!'

This time Stone looked as blank as the DC, who had long since dismissed Mrs Haverton as a twittering sparrow.

'La Coruña. So much more romantic than our anglicized Corunna. Why do we flatten foreign names? Wouldn't you much rather refer to Pillar of Heracles than Gibraltar?'

Stone smiled. 'It would take longer to write.'

'D'you know, I'd never thought of that! ... And then she'll be visiting Malaga and I don't know where else. I'd give anything to be with her. Although, of course, one's enjoyment will so much depend on what the other seven passengers are like. If one of them is truly unsympathetic, it can upset everything.'

'It doesn't sound to be very big?'

'Just a small cargo boat. Oh dear, one should never call a ship a boat, should one? I remember years ago I had to make a train journey to the Continent which lasted all day and in the same compartment was a man who simply would not stop talking ... Unfortunately, there are some people like that.'

Stone hurriedly spoke to prevent any comment from the DC. 'I'm afraid that's true.'

'My husband says that they suffer from verbal diarrhœa. Rather rude, I suppose, but so descriptive.'

They heard the thud of the front door as it was shut.

'That must be Joanna, since my husband can't possibly be back for at least another hour and I told Mrs Hepworth not to return this afternoon even though she had to leave early to see the doctor—or was it the chemist? He will work too hard, no matter what I say. That's my husband, not the doctor or the chemist.' She stood. 'I'll just tell her you're here.' She left, taking short, quick strides.

The DC said in a low voice: 'Imagine being cooped up with her on a tiny ship!'

Mrs Haverton returned, followed by Joanna who was wearing a tight-fitting T-shirt and hip-hugging jeans. 'What are you doing here?'

Joanna demanded aggressively.

'Waiting to have a word with you,' Stone replied pleasantly. 'By the way, Andy sends his regards.'

She crossed to a chair, sat. She noticed the way in which the DC was regarding her and rewarded him with a look of such supercilious dislike that he hastily turned away.

Mrs Haverton was perplexed. 'You know each other, then?'

'My son is a friend of Joanna's,' Stone replied.

'How very nice.' She was even more perplexed. When she couldn't understand a situation, she escaped from it. She stood. 'Joanna, you haven't forgotten we're out to drinks, have you?'

'Not for an hour-and-a-half.'

'I do hope Basil will be back in time. He did promise faithfully he would be, but I'm never quite certain how much he likes the Taylors ... Do you think you'll be all right if I leave you and go and change?'

'I'll scream for help at the first sign of rape.'

Mrs Haverton strongly disapproved of such a remark in mixed company; her lips were pursed as she left the room.

Stone said: 'Would you mind answering a few questions?'

'How can I tell until I hear what they are?' Joanna replied curtly.

'I'm interested in what happened last month,

after Andrew had left your house on the Saturday.'

On the piecrust table by the side of her chair was a heavily engraved silver cigarette box and lighter. She lit a cigarette.

'Can you recall that night?'

'It's a long time ago.'

'Andy had spent the evening with you.'

She smiled sarcastically.

'When he left, he walked through the courtyard and was by the gateway when a man knocked him out, obviously thinking he was a burglar.'

'Nobody could look less like one.'

'They come in all shapes and sizes. Just before he was laid out, he caught a glimpse of the man's face and from his description we've been able to identify a possible suspect. I'm hoping you'll be able to confirm that identification.'

'Why would I be able to?'

'Because he was in your house that night.' Stone brought a photograph of Illmore from his pocket, stood, and crossed to show this to Joanna. 'Do you recognize him?'

'No. And no one was in our house that night.'

'Are you quite certain?'

'I've just said so … Who the hell is he, anyway?'

'He's been using the name Roger Illmore. Earlier that night he'd escaped from prison.'

He returned to his chair and sat. 'You left home on the Sunday morning. Why was there this sudden change of plan?'

'Why not?'

'You had a date with Andy that evening.'

'So?'

'You broke it for no reason whatsoever?'

She shrugged her shoulders.

'Was it your father who suggested you came up here to stay with the Havertons?'

'Is that any concern of yours?'

'Because he didn't want you to meet Andy that evening?'

'He's not hot on my meeting him any evening.'

'Joanna, the lives of a lot of people could rest on what you tell me.'

'How dramatic!'

'People are likely to be brutally murdered if you don't tell me what you know about Illmore.'

'Talk about hypocrisy! What you're really after is to get me to say that my father hid an escaped criminal. Well, he didn't.'

'Don't you understand that there are times when one owes a duty to others that's even greater than the duty one owes one's own family?'

She came to her feet. 'You think I give a damn about a hundred unknowns if they're measured against my father? You don't know the first thing about anything.' She left.

Stone was bitterly reminded of what he had said to Kemp not so long before.

'She's one right royal bitch,' said the DC admiringly.

They left and were half way across the hall when they heard footsteps and turned. Mrs Haverton, who had not begun to change for the cocktail party, hurried across from one of the doorways. 'I do hope that everything's all right and Joanna's been able to help you?'

'Able, but unwilling,' Stone replied bluntly.

'Oh dear! She can be stubborn. Perhaps she's in a mood because she didn't like the friends in Keswick—or were they distant relatives? If you come back another day, probably you'll find her more helpful ... But of course, I'm forgetting. She's returning home on Sunday.'

'Then she's not joining the ship right away?'

'I don't think it arrives in La Coruña until some time that day and so she doesn't have to fly out until Wednesday ... I should have said, "she arrives", shouldn't I? It's so very difficult—I mean, why is a ship a she and not an it?'

'Because if she's not carefully steered, she goes round in circles,' replied Stone. As Mrs Haverton dutifully smiled, he thought that amid her verbal meanderings there might well lie a kernel of vitally important fact.

CHAPTER TWENTY-THREE

Stone spoke to Kemp over the telephone. 'No direct luck, I'm afraid. Joanna refused even to begin to discuss what happened.'

'I imagine you explained how vital her evidence could be?'

'She said, quite bluntly, that her only concern was her father.'

'Unfortunately, that was always on the cards.'

'But it may not be all failure. Mrs Haverton, with whom she's staying, would talk all four legs off a donkey; in the course of her babblings she said something which might just be significant. I realize it's one hell of a longshot...'

'This case has been about longshots.'

'Joanna's returning home on Sunday. On Wednesday she's flying to Corunna to join a small ship which carries a few passengers. It was fully booked up, but her father managed to wangle her a berth by getting another passenger bumped. It seems her father spoils her something rotten and the trip's compensation for moving her up to Cumberland so suddenly last month.'

'So what are you suggesting?'

'That if Ogilvy can have a passenger bumped in order to give his daughter a berth, he must have a great deal of clout with whoever runs that ship. That could make him a regular charterer. In which case, getting his daughter a berth at the expense of someone else may not be his only trick. If the ship's Irish registered and manned, there might be no great difficulty in persuading the crew to smuggle the LAGSSAM launchers and rockets.'

'Go on.'

'There's not much further to go. Just that if Joanna's returning home on Sunday, it must be because Ogilvy considers it's safe for her to reappear because even if she's questioned and inadvertently lets something slip, no harm will be done. The ship probably docks on Sunday.'

'What's the name of the ship and where has she sailed from?'

'I wasn't told. And I haven't liked to ask because that would make our interest very obvious.'

'Right. Get back here as quickly as you can.'

As Stone replaced the receiver, he reflected that it really was not in Kemp's nature to praise.

* * *

Kemp stared at the list of ships which had docked and would be docking at La Coruña between Thursday and Sunday. One name stood out, as if written in capital letters. MV *Flemagh*, registered in Cóbh, due on Sunday morning.

Over the phone he asked for details of her present voyage. He was told that the *Flemagh*, which had both refrigerated and dry goods capacity, had sailed from Savannah with a mixed cargo of frozen seafood and manufactured goods, bound for Spain.

It was impossible to work any longer independently of AT. He rang the detective-superintendent and had much pleasure in explaining how he and his team had turned up what might prove to be a very strong lead...

'Landing 'em in port?' said the detective-superintendent scornfully. 'You don't know much about the way these bastards work. Bribe a Customs man today and tomorrow he'll be shopping you. The crew will off-load 'em at sea at night, to be picked up by a fishing-boat that'll slip into a cove and unload 'em in minutes.'

'Then we'd better get someone...'

'I'll handle this from now on.'

*   *   *

There was no need to initiate a hunt for the *Flemagh* in order to pinpoint her before she closed the coast. Twice a day, at 0800 and 2000 hours GMT, she made a meteorological report by radio and this included her DR position. With these, it was a simple task to work out her average speed and probable course to La

230

Coruña.

An ancient Nimrod, converted from its original purpose to that of maritime watchdog and equipped with downlooking radar, very high resolution and night image intensifying scopes, and cameras that from 30,000 feet could catch the wink of the unicorn's eye on a one-pound coin, kept the *Flemagh* under surveillance from the moment she came within two hundred miles of Cape Finisterre.

When she was just under fifty miles out, radar picked up a second vessel which closed. 'Here comes the drop,' said the pilot, who was an old hand.

He was right.

*   *   *

The phone rang. Moving slowly and carefully, since many parts of her body could still cause considerable pain and she had not yet accustomed herself to the cast on her leg, June thumped her way into the hall and answered the call. The DI wanted her husband in his office, now. She returned to the kitchen and opened the outside door. 'Gerry, the station's just rung. Mr Kemp wants you.'

He straightened up from the ever-recalcitrant mower. 'I'll wash and get going, then.' He gave the mower a kick out of habit, crossed to the doorway.

'You will be back to lunch, won't you?'

231

'When you've cooked your special cottage pie that should be called manor pie?' He knew that she was envisaging him in a cell, facing a lunch of bread and water.

'Gerry ... Oh God, Gerry!' She reached out to him.

He held her tightly. 'There's no call for panic, love. Didn't you read your horoscope this morning? It said that you're in for a pleasant surprise.'

'You know it didn't mention anything about pleasant.'

'Horoscope surprises are obliged by law to be pleasant.' He gave her a hug, gently released her, eased past and went inside to wash his hands in the sink. When he kissed her goodbye, she clung to him for several seconds.

In the car park at divisional HQ the only free parking space was that which was reserved for the superintendent. He drove into it. The condemned man was allowed his last pathetic act of defiance.

The DI, seated at his desk, had his coat off and hung on the back of the chair. 'Grab a seat ... First off, you'll want to hear the results of the operation. The boat which picked up the drop was intercepted a mile off the Irish coast. In addition to a good catch of fish, she was carrying three LAGSSAM launchers, twelve rockets, and Illmore so seasick that he couldn't even reach for the gun under the pillow.'

There was silence, which Stone broke. 'It's

232

odd, isn't it? If I hadn't tried to cover up the evidence of the hit-and-run, none of this would have come to light.'

'I once read that God must have an ironic sense of humour.'

There was another silence. 'There's nothing through from the lab yet on the paint?' Stone asked.

'I was coming to that. Their report was in this morning's post.'

He found difficulty in speaking. 'So I'm finally nailed?'

'The tests have shown that the comparison paint almost matches the crime sample, but there is discrepancy—very small, yet just sufficient to prevent an identification strong enough for the courts. They suggest that the comparison sample was taken from a point at which very light touching-up had previously been carried out; since there was no obvious indication of this, else paint would have been taken from another point on the car, this was probably a factory blemish, noted by a quality inspector, and dealt with before the car left. Whichwayever, the lab has asked for another comparison sample to be taken from a different part of your car.'

Stone stared blankly into space. 'Another three weeks waiting for the inevitable? June won't be able to take that.'

'Why d'you think she'll have to?'

'Because you've just said ...'

'Aren't you forgetting something? Your car was bombed and burned out. There's not enough paint left on the wreck to cover a pinhead. So no more tests can be carried out and the law, which in its wisdom demands certainty, not probability, is going to have to go unsatisfied.'

Out of an act of terror had come salvation. A very ironic sense of humour, Stone thought, as Catherine wheels began to spin in his mind.